Shortchanged

Shortchanged

John H. Harding, Jr.

BRANDYLANE PUBLISHERS
White Stone, Virginia

 Brandylane Publishers

P.O. Box 261, White Stone, Virginia 22578
(804) 435-6900 or 1 800 553-6922; e-mail: brandy@crosslink.net

Back cover photo credit: the old jail in Heathsville, Virginia—Karen Martin Harding

Library of Congress Cataloging-in-Publication Data

Harding, John H., Jr., 1929–
   Shortchanged/John Harding
     p. cm.
   ISBN 1–883911–22–2
   1. Korean War, 1950–1953—Fiction. I. Title.
PS3558.A62328S57   1998
813'.54—dc21   97–51124
                                                CIP

To Karen

Acknowledgments

I wish to thank my wife, Karen Martin Harding, without whose help and support this work would not have been completed.

I especially want to thank Mr. Richard Maxwell for his encouragement and for reading the manuscript and making suggestions.

Also, I wish to thank the Wednesday Book Group for having me preview the book for them, and especially Mrs. Ada Clark Davis for suggesting the title.

I want to thank my daughter, Leannah Mason Harding, for deciphering my handwriting and willingly typing my manuscript, chapter by chapter, into the computer. And thanks to her husband, Paul Chernoff, for his computer expertise.

As with any book, proper editing is essential. I was most fortunate in having the best. Beth Boone Bradford did a remarkable job.

I want to express my appreciation to Mr. Robert Pruett for agreeing to publish this, my first book, and to the staff of Brandylane Publishers for their help.

Chapter One

There was no sun, but the rain had turned to mist. It covered my glasses so I couldn't see and made my face feel as if I was sweating. Mostly, it was cold.

Snow covered the mountain tops to my left and right, and heavy clouds gave the hint of more snow on the way.

I looked around, left to right. For as far as I could see, rocks stuck out of the ground with dead grass tucked here and there at the base of the outcroppings. There were no birds or animals. Not even an insect. I closed my eyes and listened. A shell whined overhead. Then there was a dull explosion. It seemed to be miles away.

I tried to move my left foot, but it was numb. I wrapped both hands around my left knee and forced the leg to move. It hurt more than I want to remember, but the numbness soon faded. How long had I been there? It seemed like days. How had I gotten there? For that matter, why was I there?

I put my head back and banged my helmet against something hard. A rock, I thought, but it didn't hurt. My helmet liner had cushioned the blow.

"Quiet!" The voice was sharp, but I knew it. And then I remembered. . .

I was in the U.S. Army. It was 1951, and I had been sent

to Korea. The events of the day and night before began to form in my mind. I thought if I held my head still and opened my eyes wide, l could recollect all of it.

Captain Wood, who was the battalion S-2, had gotten all of us—Lieutenant Brown, Sergeant Kelly and myself—together. He said we were going to establish an observation post. We were to pack enough supplies for seven days. He said this meant food, water, our winter gear and our radio equipment. He told us not to bother with telephone equipment.

The days before this had been pleasant enough. We were bivouacked in some fairly safe place and had hot food, hot water, and several hot showers. I had gotten two letters from home. That was the best part, and during the week, sleeping on a cot in a tent with five other men and a heater wasn't so bad.

The captain said we were to leave in a jeep about one and a half hours before dark. Sergeant Kelly and I loaded everything in the jeep, and we were ready to go. I had even bought a new can of lighter fluid for my pocket warmer from one of the men in my tent. Lieutenant Brown checked to see if we had everything ready. He told us he was on his way to artillery headquarters to get our mission and see what else he could find out. He said we would leave when he got back.

The weather was cloudy, but at least it wasn't raining or snowing. I figured the temperature was in the high thirties. At home in Virginia on a winter afternoon like this we would expect snow. We were waiting near the jeep. It was parked near a bush and covered with camouflage net.

A while later Lieutenant Brown came back from HQ and asked if we were ready. Sergeant Kelly nodded. I said, "Yes, Sir," and the lieutenant brought out a map and laid it on the hood of the jeep.

"We will report to infantry battalion headquarters. From there we are to go through infantry lines and establish an

2

observation post." He told us we would end up a mile or two in front of the infantry. We would be in no man's land.

Sergeant Kelly looked at Lieutenant Brown. I could tell by his expression that this was bad news. I was new to Korea, but even I knew why no telephone equipment was needed. This was the plan: We would leave our jeep near infantry battalion headquarters and walk through the lines where the infantry units were dug in. We were to go to a hill about one mile from the nearest infantry unit and dig in. We would do this at night.

I tried to see the hill number, but Sergeant Kelly's finger blocked it. The army gave hills numbers, not names. The number was the hill's height above sea level. Sometimes, a unit that had fought there would name a hill, but otherwise, no names, just numbers.

Lieutenant Brown was anxious to go. He wanted to get through the infantry lines by dark. He said if not we would risk getting shot by our own troops. Sergeant Kelly and I pulled the net off the jeep and left it in a pile on the ground. Someone else could pick it up. Sergeant Kelly got in the driver's seat, Lieutenant Brown sat in the passenger seat, and I got in the back with the equipment and food.

Lieutenant Brown tapped Sergeant Kelly's shoulder, "Is the gas tank full?"

Sergeant Kelly nodded. "But I didn't get an extra gas can."

"I don't think we'll need it," Lieutenant Brown said.

The jeep top was down, but the windshield was up, and as we started, a mist formed on it. It looked as if it was going to rain or snow in the mountains, but we kept going. There were no roads to follow, only tracks where vehicles had been. I felt good, all warm, as I snuggled down into the equipment and gear. And the gear made the bumps easier to bear. In the front seats Lieutenant Brown looked at his map and told Sergeant Kelly where to go.

The wind began to blow from what I thought was the

3

north, and then the rain began to fall. Occasionally flakes of snow were mixed with the rain. I shivered. I wished I had lit my pocket warmer. It would have felt good to my hands. I had them clenched into fists and stuffed in my pockets, but they were cold anyway. I dozed off and on as we bumped along the muddy tracks, occasionally veering to the right or left. In some of the tracks there was standing water; in others I saw some ice from the last freeze.

I could tell by the mountains on either side that we were following a valley, but I didn't know for sure in which direction we were traveling. My geography was not the best. I had only gone to school for parts of eight years. I had to work setting tomato plants and doing yard work to help support my mother. In basic training they had said I was smart. They said I got good scores on the tests they gave at the induction center. I always wondered what they knew about me from the tests. Like did my answers tell them anything about how I would do here. Maybe they told me I was smart so I would do what I was told. I didn't like trouble. I knew that, having been in neighborhood fights as a young boy. Also, I had seen people get in trouble with the sergeant in basic training. I didn't plan on being an example for anyone else, so I did what I was told.

As we rode along, the rain turned completely to snow that got heavier and began sticking to the ground. All I could think about was that it was sure going to be cold up on that hill.

Before long, we approached four soldiers who were facing us. Two were kneeling, one was on his stomach, and the other was standing. Lieutenant Brown told Sergeant Kelly to slow down and then stop after pulling off to the left. These soldiers had their M1 rifles trained on us. To my right, I could make out a machine gun barrel. The barrel was all I could see. Lieutenant Brown got out of the jeep and yelled something. It was probably some password, but I was not paying much attention. I was watching that machine gun. I didn't like someone pointing a gun at me. I knew it was

4

loaded, and I knew the safety was off.

As Lieutenant Brown talked, the two kneeling soldiers rose to their feet. The soldier who had been standing pointed to the left. I figured he was indicating where we were supposed to go. The Lieutenant sat back in the jeep. He spoke real low. "They were expecting us." He said they hadn't thought we would get here by dark.

The soldier who was on his stomach seemed to slide from sight. I figured he slid back into his foxhole.

The standing soldier picked up a field telephone. As he was talking on the phone, he turned and I could see the sergeant's stripes on his helmet. I heard him say that the observation party had arrived. It didn't seem like a big deal to me. And then a young PFC came out of a camouflaged tent and waved his hands at us.

"What do you think he wants?" Sergeant Kelly asked.

"Wait here, I'll find out," said Lieutenant Brown. He got out of the jeep again real slowly as if he were stiff from the cold and bumpy ride.

I couldn't hear what was being said, but with a swift turn and an arm signal, Lieutenant Brown motioned that the jeep was to be parked nearby. Sergeant Kelly drove the jeep where the young soldier indicated and told him we didn't have our own camouflage net. The young soldier disappeared and came back with the netting. Lieutenant Brown instructed us to unload the jeep, get all our equipment and gear together and stay in this area. He said he was going to infantry battalion headquarters to find out exactly where we were to go.

When Lieutenant Brown returned a few minutes later, he told us what he had found out. I was scared to hear what he said. As soon as the weather cleared, we could expect an attack by the enemy. It was our mission to get to Hill 4413 undetected. We were to stay seven days, and then be replaced.

Most important, he said, was this. We were not to give

a radio signal until the enemy began to move. We were not to signal for any other reason. Headquarters would monitor our radio at all times.

Lieutenant Brown went on to say there was an artillery observation post about one mile from our intended position on Hill 4413. Headquarters believed the enemy knew the location of that observation post. He said the infantry battalion would send a patrol out with us. One of its missions was to help us with our equipment and gear. He also said there were enemy patrols in the area. We were to avoid all contact if possible.

Lieutenant Brown asked if we had any questions. My mouth flew open, but I couldn't seem to speak. What I wanted to ask was, "What am I doing here?" I had been trained as a driver. Since Sergeant Kelly had done the driving from the rear area, and since we were to walk the long distance to the summit of Hill 4413, I certainly wasn't needed as a driver.

"What time do we leave?" Sergeant Kelly asked.

Lieutenant Brown said we would eat something and then move out. He said we would walk in the dark. It would be uphill over rocky terrain.

There was still a fine mist in the air, but the snow had stopped temporarily. I could feel the fear rising in my throat. I tried to swallow, but I couldn't. Here we were, going off into no man's land, through our own lines, stumbling along in the dark over a bunch of rocks. And it would probably be snowing. What did this have to do with me? I was a driver. To tell the truth, I really wasn't worrying about the enemy patrols. I thought maybe they had more sense than to be out on a night like this.

Sergeant Kelly called to me and motioned that I should come with him to get something to eat. Lieutenant Brown left, probably to eat with the officers.

It wasn't long before we were back at the spot where we had unloaded the jeep. Our gear, equipment, and food were where we had left them. Our equipment consisted of one radio and some spare batteries. Lieutenant Brown had given Sergeant Kelly our assigned frequencies. I hoped he had written them down.

We also had two pair of field glasses and a BC scope, an instrument we used to see over long distances. Of course, we had our carbines and ammo. The rest of our gear consisted of food—cans of meat and fruit and crackers. It wasn't very good, but you could eat it okay. We also had cans of water, ponchos, tents, blankets, and a shovel to dig our foxholes.

In those last moments before sunset and complete darkness, four men approached us. Their leader, a tall heavy-set man with a mustache, saluted Lieutenant Brown.

"Your accompanying patrol reporting. We'll help you get to the summit of Hill 4413." He asked what his men could carry and they divided up our load. As we walked, I listened to the conversation between Lieutenant Brown and the patrol leader. Lieutenant Brown asked if he had been to Hill 4413.

"No," he said, "but I have been close to the area on patrol. This will be a difficult walk, especially in the dark." He told Lieutenant Brown we needed to get there in time to dig foxholes before daylight. Otherwise we should stay on this side of the summit.

This confused me at first, but then it made sense. If we couldn't dig foxholes on the far side of the summit by daylight, then we'd wait till dark the next night. We did not want to be seen by the enemy, but to get the best view of the enemy, we would have to be just below the summit on the enemy's side.

The patrol leader's name was Smith. He was a master sergeant. He turned to me and asked, "Are you a coal miner?"

"No, Sergeant," I said.

He turned to one of the men going on patrol. "Hand me that pick." The man produced a short-handled pick. It was the kind of pick I had seen gold miners using in movies. "That rock will be hard to dig a foxhole in," the master sergeant said. He handed me the pick, adding with a twinkle in his eye, "I want that pick back."

This was comforting to me. It meant he thought we'd get back safe and sound. I had seen this type of sergeant before. They were the backbone of the army. A lot of people said that about sergeants, but with guys like Master Sergeant Smith, the saying was true. They were the people who got things done. They knew the army; they also knew how their men felt—afraid. I remembered having a similar master sergeant in basic training. We carried our weapons in the sling position on marches. He taught us how to get our weapons from sling position into firing position quickly. A tale was told—how true it was I didn't know—about him being on patrol and coming face-to-face with a Japanese patrol. He was able to get three shots off before the Japanese could get their weapons into firing position.

With the master sergeant accompanying us, I felt more relaxed as we loaded up our equipment and gear. I was ready to start out on the long walk to Hill 4413.

Chapter Two

We walked along with Lieutenant Brown in front, followed by Sergeant Smith. The lieutenant told us to remove the safeties on our guns. Each of us had a full magazine in our carbines except for Sergeant Smith, who had his service revolver in his right hand and a plastic-covered map in his left hand.

"We're close to the front lines," Sergeant Smith told the lieutenant. We knew the front lines would be manned by squads in foxholes. They would be located along our route in strategic positions. Foxholes were all well dug, and then had sand bags piled on three sides and across the top. These, we knew, were held up by boards from shell case boxes, logs, or any other materials that the soldiers could find. The holes were dug about three feet deep. There was a gap in the sand bags in the front and slightly to each side so the men could see in those directions.

Sergeant Smith said the men manning the positions knew we would be passing through. Having Sergeant Smith with us gave us a good feeling. If we could safely get to Hill 4413, the sergeant would get us there.

The holes we passed were well camouflaged, but we could feel those soldiers around us. Lieutenant Brown told

Sergeant Smith to take the lead. I thought this was a good idea. The sergeant had been on patrol in the area before.

Sergeant Smith told the lieutenant to pass the word: no talking, and stay close. I was third in line, near the front of our group, I guess, because I carried the radio.

It was dark now and I could feel the mist on my face. Was this a fine snow, or was it rain? What difference did it make? We were going anyway. As we walked, I stumbled over rocks, but I kept going and I kept quiet. I tried to think that this was like the 'coon hunting I used to do with a boy in my neighborhood back in Virginia.

We each had pet dogs that slept in the house with us. They weren't purebred hunting dogs but mixtures, and they were our good friends. We usually took our dogs around the edge of a cornfield at night, after the corn had been harvested. We wore high rubber boots which were necessary because the furrows near the edges of the field were usually half full of water. One of us would carry a kerosene lantern. Of course, the dogs barked at almost anything, including shadows, and we would holler for them to "go get 'em." The dogs always barked and ran here and there. I don't remember them chasing a raccoon up a tree, but on occasion we would come across a 'possum playing dead. The dogs were always interested at first, but when the animal didn't run, they lost interest.

But one time the dogs started barking, and we finally caught up with them and shone our light into the woods. We could see they had treed a cat. We called off the dogs by taking each by its collar and petting it and telling it not to chase the cat. Of course, the dogs didn't know what to chase, or when, as they weren't trained hunting dogs.

I stumbled again, almost falling. Sergeant Smith must have seen me because he slowed and passed the word back to stop. I gladly sat down and removed the straps that held the radio case. My feet ached, not so much from the distance, but from walking on rocky ground. I had always considered myself to be tough though, so I knew I could take as much as anybody else. We knew we weren't to talk or make unnecessary noise. And I was sure Sergeant Smith was listening for an enemy patrol. I knew these stops would become more numerous as we got farther from the American lines.

Moments later, Sergeant Smith ordered us to move out. I felt for the radio equipment straps and slipped them onto my shoulder. When we started off again, we moved more rapidly. There were fewer rocks, and it was easier to keep my footing. We must have been directly behind Hill 4413 because the wind had died down, but the mist had turned to snow.

Sergeant Smith had us stop often. At each stop, he would look at his compass and map with a small flashlight, that had its lens mostly covered with paint. At the same time I was sure he was listening for any sound, as we all were. At last he told Lieutenant Brown that we had reached the base of Hill 4413.

I had always thought I had good night vision. In basic training we had to walk from one hill to another at night. We did this in groups of four. Each of us had a flashlight, compass, and map like Sergeant Smith. One of the four in my group kept telling me he couldn't see at night. I told him if he hooked my belt loop with his finger I would lead him along. I always got him from one hill to another this way.

We had begun to climb the hill. As we walked along slowly, each step seemed to be at least six inches higher than the last, but the pace was slow with so many stops and starts. I wasn't sleepy, but in the dark and quiet it was easy to think.

The barracks was the only building I had ever lived in that had electric lights. Each night as the sun was going down, my mother would light the kerosene lamp that we ate our supper by. We heated hot water in a pan on our stove all year long. One of my jobs was to keep the wood box filled. When I was small, my mother used to help me, but by the time I was six I could handle the ax well enough to cut the wood and bring it into the house by myself. I never did much homework for school. I was usually too tired. When we had finished supper and my mother had washed the dishes, I would climb the narrow turning stairs to my room over the kitchen. My dog usually lay by the stove, especially when it was cold. When my mother was ready to go to bed she would let my dog out, and then back in, and the dog would come up the stairs and slip under the covers with me.

Lieutenant Brown tugged at my arm. We had stopped again, but this time when I looked up at the sky I could see light. There was a break in the clouds, and the moon shone for a few seconds. We were near the top of a hill. Off to our left and right there were taller hills covered with snow. Where we stood, it seemed colder, but there was no snow on the ground. Maybe it was the sight of snow on the distant hills, but I shivered.

Sergeant Smith told Lieutenant Brown this was as far as his patrol would go, but he said they would help us store our equipment and supplies. I knew what this meant. We would dig holes and camouflage them.

"How long before daylight?" the lieutenant asked Sergeant Smith.

"About three hours."

The lieutenant asked the sergeant what he thought would be the best plan of action. I couldn't hear the answer, but it didn't matter. The army teaches you that the officer makes all the decisions, and the non-commissioned officer sees that they are carried out. I was just glad to see that the lieutenant had sense enough to ask Sergeant Smith, who was experienced with this type of operation, what was best to do. Lieutenant Brown seemed like a nice enough guy. He was a product of the ROTC, but I didn't know what college he had attended. Not that the name would mean much to me anyway.

A few minutes later, the lieutenant took Sergeant Kelly

and me aside. He said Sergeant Smith and his men would dig two foxholes, one for equipment, and one for supplies, on this side of the crest of Hill 4413. Sergeant Kelly and I would go with the lieutenant over the crest and start digging our positions there. We would leave our equipment and supplies in a pile and carry only carbines and shovels to the other side. In my belt I had the miner's pick Sergeant Smith had given to me earlier that evening.

The moon broke through the clouds again, so we waited until it was hidden before we climbed over the crest of the hill. Lieutenant Brown quickly picked the spot he thought would be best for our observation post. There were two large rocks. We would dig the foxhole behind them. I thought maybe we could move some smaller rocks and put them on each side. This would make for less digging.

I took my shovel and pushed it into the ground. It went in easily for about four inches, then hit something hard. I tried several places, but each time, my shovel hit rock just under the ground. Lieutenant Brown stood for a moment looking around at the rocks. Sergeant Kelly whispered that it would be hard digging, and I took off my helmet. I thought if I used it as a scoop to get the loose dirt out of the hole I was trying to make, I might make some progress.

Meanwhile, the lieutenant went back over the crest of the hill to check on the patrol's progress. When he returned, he said Sergeant Smith and his patrol had finished by the time he got there, and now they had left. They had found an easy place to dig and all of our equipment and supplies were secured. The lieutenant said Sergeant Smith had wished us luck. He had told the lieutenant, "Once you see the enemy coming, send your message, and get the hell out of there." This, to put it mildly, sounded like good advice to me.

Sergeant Kelly and I continued to dig. The lieutenant told me to put my helmet back on and to use my shovel. With the help of the pick we soon had a decent-sized hole, with good cover on all sides. Then the lieutenant told us it

13

would soon be light. He said we should get the radio and BC scope set up and camouflage our position. As we did this, I wondered if the radio would work, and if we had the right frequencies. After we finished, Lieutenant Brown said Sergeant Kelly and I should go back over the crest, find the foxholes that Sergeant Smith's men had dug, and get some sleep. He would man the observation post for the first watch. I told the lieutenant where I left the pick—to the right of the radio. I knew from training that we would continue to improve our position by digging deeper and improving our camouflage for as long as we occupied this post.

It didn't take long for the sergeant and me to get back over the crest of the hill and find the holes the patrol had dug. There was no moon now; maybe it had set. As I wrapped myself in a blanket and covered it with a poncho, I slid my helmet down over my eyes very gently to keep it from hitting the rocks behind me. Was I scared? Yes, I was, but what could I do? We had gotten to Hill 4413, and we were dug in.

I was with a good crew, but still, what was a driver doing in this position? What if the enemy came? What if there was a big battle? I prayed the enemy would stay away. Then I thought about my mother and about a girl I had met while I was in basic training.

Chapter Three

I had fallen asleep. When I awoke, my poncho and blanket had fallen off, and I was cold! The barrel of my carbine was exposed, so I slipped my poncho over it to keep it dry. Being right-handed I was taught to sleep with the carbine on my right side so I could get to it quickly. I guess left-handed people slept with their weapons on their left sides. I rubbed my hands together and wiggled my toes to keep the blood moving. It was the only way I could stay warm.

"You awake?" Sergeant Kelly asked in a low voice.

"Yes," I said.

"We should eat and relieve the lieutenant," he said.

I asked where the chow was.

"Cans on the way!" With that, I saw him toss three cans into the air above me. I tried to catch them, but my hands got caught up in the blanket, and the cans cracked against the rocks. I grabbed them quickly.

The sergeant said we would use a can of Heet to warm the next meal, but now he thought we should get to the observation post and let the lieutenant get some sleep. He had been up all night.

I opened my first can without looking at the label. It contained crackers, and I knew from experience that they

15

tasted pretty good but were real dry. I went to check my equipment belt to be sure I had my canteen, but my belt had disappeared. I felt panicky because my ammo had been attached to my belt, as well. I threw the blanket aside and stood up. I was really relieved to find my belt.

My carbine was still lying in the corner of the foxhole where I had covered it with the poncho. I put the belt around my waist and fastened it, being as quiet as I could. Then I removed my canteen and opened it, putting it between my knees. The next can I opened was fruit cocktail. Holding the can of fruit to my lips I drank the juice. I took a cracker and broke it and dipped a corner of the cracker into the can of fruit. It tasted good, but even with the fruit on it, the cracker was dry. After I chewed and swallowed, I needed a drink, which I took from my canteen.

Just then a shell flew over our heads. It came from the direction we had traveled to get here. "Those shells you hear won't hurt you," the sergeant said in a reassuring voice. In a few seconds, the shell exploded. Within a minute, another shell flew over our heads and exploded. It was closer than the first.

"What's going on?" Sergeant Kelly whispered, curious to find out how much I knew.

"I don't have any idea," I said, "but it seems to me our own artillery is trying to shell this hill."

He chuckled and leaned over to my foxhole. His was separated from mine by about a foot of dirt and rock. He said, "Let me explain what's going on. One artillery battery is registering."

I had no idea what he was talking about. After all, I was trained as a driver. But I decided to try to understand what the sergeant was telling me.

"Each artillery battery has six guns, which can be different sizes. I think this battery has 105 mm Howitzers."

"How do you know?"

"From the size of the explosion. It could also be a

155 mm or a 75 mm. The larger the gun, the larger the explosion."

"But how can you tell?"

"When you hear enough of them you can tell."

Back at Fort Sill I had heard the boys talk about different size guns, but I was training to be a driver, and didn't pay much attention. At Fort Sill I learned to drive a jeep and a 2 1/2 ton truck.

One thing that always puzzled me was why I was picked to be a driver. I had never driven a vehicle until I was in the army. One time my brother had let me steer his car while he was driving. Another time he let me start it up and showed me how to change gears, but I never actually drove.

"Weather conditions change," said Sergeant Kelly. "Temperature, humidity, barometric pressure, wind speed and direction change. The same gun, with its elevation and direction settings and the same powder charge, will fire its projectile a greater or lesser distance every time because of these changes. Also, its projectile will go more to the right or left depending on the change of conditions. They register in order to be able to apply corrections for current conditions."

We were talking almost in a whisper, And the shells continued to fly over our heads and explode.

"How many shells does it take to register?" I asked.

"There is a forward observer from the artillery battery with the infantry battalion. The forward observer picks a target on the map and sends its location to the battery. The battery fire control officer figures the direction and distance from the battery and from a prepared table is able to estimate the correct powder charge and elevation of the barrel."

"How did you learn so much about artillery?" I asked.

"I worked in an artillery fire control center, and I've been with forward observers. They may fire several rounds to see if the shells land short or long of the target. The number of shells fired depends on the ammo supply and the need for keeping gun positions as secret as possible."

I thought this was very interesting. While the sergeant was talking I had finished my fruit cocktail and opened a can of meat. I don't know what it was, but it didn't taste like anything I had eaten before. I ate it anyway.

Sergeant Kelly asked if I was ready, and I nodded. He said to bring my carbine, poncho, and blanket and to crawl, staying as close to the ground as I could. He said he would lead the way. As I crawled out of the foxhole, I had a weird feeling of sudden peril, but I was glad I was with Sergeant Kelly and Lieutenant Brown.

Chapter Four

I crawled as close to the ground as I could, but I kept thinking my butt was high in the air. I had my arms full, so couldn't do much pulling with my elbows or hands. Ahead of me I saw Sergeant Kelly. His butt was low to the ground, so I tried harder to get mine down as much as I could.

The wind was picking up and hitting me right in the face. Luckily, I had my wool cap under my helmet liner. It would keep my ears warm. My ears always got cold. Mother had made me the cap and given it to me when I was home on my last leave. It was the only piece of clothing my mother had ever made for me.

I heard the sergeant calling to Lieutenant Brown. I couldn't hear what he said, but got enough of the conversation to know the lieutenant was going to the rear to sleep. The sergeant and I were to move to the observation post.

Lieutenant Brown crawled out of the foxhole and past the sergeant. When he got up to me, he said with a smile, "Kid, keep your eyes open and your head down." I dug my feet in and crawled to the edge of the foxhole.

Sergeant Kelly was already in the small hole. He was looking through the Battery Commander's telescope. He whispered, "Come on in." We arranged the camouflage net so we were completely covered. The foxhole was crowded, but it did cut some of the wind. I asked the sergeant what he wanted me to do.

"Nothing right now." He continued looking through the BC scope. After a few minutes he asked if I knew how to operate the radio. I said I did.

"Have you ever looked through a BC scope?"

"No."

He moved to one side and said, "Take a look." He showed me how to adjust the focus and how to adjust it to use both eyes. I was disappointed at what I could see. Nothing. He said I should take my glasses off.

I used the adjustments and could see things at great distance in minute detail. He also showed me which knob to use to move the head of the scope around. He pointed out certain landmarks and at the same time showed me these things on the map. If there was evidence of an attack, he wanted us to get the information back to headquarters and get the "H" out of there as soon as we could.

After I had about two hours practice using the instrument and reading the map, the sergeant told me to take a nap. I reached in the pocket of my field jacket and took out a candy bar. I offered him half. He took it, and thanked me kindly. Before I curled up, I asked him if we should dig the hole any larger.

"Not until after dark."

The hole was crowded, but I felt secure with the rocks around it.

And then I thought, if we were watching the hills to our north, didn't the enemy also had people watching us? I had a hard time falling asleep. When I was little, my mother used to tell me stories to help me go to sleep. Now I was grown up and maybe my mother needed someone to help her. In her last letter, she said she was thinking about moving to North Carolina to be near my brother and his wife.

I had only seen my brother's wife twice. My brother Joe was married in North Carolina after World War II. His wife's name was Charlotte. They came to Virginia to visit me and my mother soon after they were married, but they only stayed one night. Although Charlotte seemed to be nice, I don't think she liked the way we lived. We had no running water, no inside plumbing, and no electric current. Our radio had a battery. We heated our house with several wood stoves called King Heaters. Mother cooked on a kerosene cook stove. It had a tank on one side that held about one gallon of kerosene. Back then people called kerosene "coal oil."

I used to go to the store and buy coal oil for two cents a gallon. Because our oil can held one and a half gallons, Mother used to let the oil run out so we could put a whole gallon in at a time. We used coal oil to start a fire in the wood stoves too, including the wood cook stove which we used only in the wintertime.

When I was small, my mother used to warn me not to put too much oil in the stove before I lit it. My mother taught me to make a fire in the stove by first putting in some paper. We didn't get a newspaper, but a woman named Mrs. Taylor used to save her papers for my mother. After Mother had read them, we used them to help start the fire. Once I had gotten several sheets of paper balled up and stuffed in the front of the stove, I would put in several pieces of kindling. Usually this was some dry pine split in small pieces. I put the kindling on top of the paper. Then I put several larger pieces of dry wood on top of the kindling.

If there were coals, left from the last fire, it could catch on its own. Or if the wood was real dry, I could light the paper by opening the draft at the bottom of the front of the stove, and it would usually begin to burn. If the wood was damp—and it usually was in the wintertime—I would pour coal oil on the wood. If it didn't light from the coals, I would strike a match and stick it in the draft at the bottom of the front of the stove. When the oil began to burn, the stove would shake and I could see fire coming out of the draft. If I hadn't gotten some of the pipe joints tight, and if I had put too much oil on the fire, flames would shoot out through these joints.

This was what happened when my brother Joe and his wife were visiting. I think it scared her. I always hoped this was not the reason they spent only one night, but maybe they only planned to stay one night. I was a just a kid. I wanted to impress my brother and sister-in-law by showing them how well I was taking care of my mother. I often hoped—and dreamed—that someday we would be able to have a better built house with running water and electricity. . .

I felt like I had just gone to sleep when I heard the sergeant calling my name.

"Are you going to sleep all day?"

"How long have I been asleep?"

"Oh, about two hours."

I couldn't believe it, but when I tried to move my legs and feet, I found they were still asleep. The sergeant said I could watch for a while. He was going to take a nap. He instructed me to wake him immediately if I saw anything unusual at all.

I felt very important knowing I was doing the observing while the other two were asleep. Imagine me, I thought, a driver dug in on the top of rocky Hill 4413.

Chapter Five

The longer I sat there on the hard rocks looking through the BC scope, the more important I felt. Here I was, doing what the sergeant and the lieutenant were trained to do. Maybe the army wasn't so bad. Maybe when my time was up, I would re-up. There were good people in the army, I thought, people like Lieutenant Brown and Sergeant Kelly.

Of course, there were people who weren't too nice, also, but you had them everywhere. The army just might have some of these not-too-nice people over you, telling you what to do, but I guessed that was the way life was anywhere. Besides I was young and had the rest of my life ahead of me. The more I thought about what I wanted to do in life, the more I didn't know. The army might be good for a career or maybe I could go back home to the Northern Neck of Virginia and get a job. Or maybe I could go to school and learn a trade. Everyone was talking about the GI bill.

I had a lot to think about, but right then I also had a lot to do. I had to look to see if there was any movement near the far hill which was brown with an outcropping of rocks. As I looked around with the BC scope, I thought again about maybe making the Army my life's work. I could maybe go to OCS and be like the lieutenant here. He seemed okay. Or

I could be an NCO like Sergeant Kelly, or like Sergeant Jones at basic training.

He was tough, or so we had heard. One of the boys from my battery got into trouble with the first sergeant, Sergeant Jones. The fellow did not do what the sergeant said to do, and they had a little discussion about it. Later in the barracks, we heard what had happened. The sergeant, with the approval of the battery commander, decided that this fellow should dig a hole. Someone would put trash in the hole and then the private would fill it up again. This didn't sound so bad until we heard that he had to use his GI shovel and dig a hole in the rocky ground that was six feet deep, four feet wide, and six feet long. He had to do all the work after duty hours, and the sergeant stayed with him, watching him while he dug. I guess this was so none of the other boys would help him. The hole was out of sight of the headquarters and barracks, but it was near the motor pool, where men worked on the trucks and jeeps.

The motor pool backed up to the woods, so the truth was nobody saw exactly what was happening. I had as much chance as anybody to see what was going on, but I didn't see anything. The boys in the barracks asked me about it one day because one of my duties was to wash the trucks and jeeps after they came in from the field, and sometimes I drove a jeep or light truck out into the field to take supplies somewhere, or to drive an officer.

As I understood it, the private only had three days to dig his hole. Well, anyway, when the hole was dug, the sergeant took a rolled up newspaper and tossed it into the hole. Then he told the fellow to fill it up. He said this newspaper had to be buried real deep.

Well, you can bet we all got the point. The rest of the time I was there, I never heard of anybody not getting along with Sergeant Jones. When he told somebody to do something, there was no question about it. We did it without hesitation. I guess we were thinking of the deep hole and all the rocks that were in the ground.

No matter how much I watched through the BC scope, I didn't see anything unusual. Nothing but a patch of snow here and there, and the rocks between the hills and the gray sky. I watched real carefully, I wanted to do a good job for the lieutenant and the sergeant. The lieutenant reminded me a little of another lieutenant I had met. His name was Lieutenant Ford. He was one of the panel of officers when I had to do guard duty at a court martial.

It was a cold damp morning as we stood in formation. Through the mist, I saw the barracks and other buildings on the far side of the drill field. The routine was the same as every day. The battalion officer of the day called the troops to attention and asked each battery officer for his report. It was always routine. "All present and accounted for." That was followed by the familiar, "Battery officers take charge of your batteries."

It was routine for the battery officer to call for the first sergeant and tell him to take charge. The first sergeant then said, "Fall out." That meant we could go to the mess hall to eat. I was always ready to eat, and the food was good. There was a sign at the beginning of the line that said, "Take what you want, but eat what you take." And I always did.

But this particular morning, the first sergeant called me and one other fellow and told us to see him after we fell out. I had no idea what I had done or hadn't done. I really didn't bother about the other boy. I knew him by name, but that was about it. As soon as we were dismissed, we hurried to the first sergeant. He told us that we had been selected to be guards at a court-martial. It would take place that morning and it might last most of the day. He told us as soon as we ate, we should go back to the barracks and put on our dress uniforms with shoes polished and pants creased so sharply they would cut his finger. Then we were supposed to report back to him. He assured us he would tell us everything to do, and dismissed us. Except he did tell us to hurry up and eat. I didn't know how we could eat right away because now we were at the end of the line. He must have guessed what I was thinking because he said, smiling, "Follow me."

He led us in the front door of the mess hall. We entered a room where the officers and noncommissioned officers ate that was separate from the place where we ate. They were served by one of the people on KP, or by one of the cooks. The first sergeant told the mess sergeant to feed us first, that we had special duty. The line was ready to move as we arrived, and we were first in line. That sure did make us feel important. We ate our breakfast real fast and hurried to the barracks. We had brushed our teeth and washed and were putting on our dress uniforms when the first of the other boys came back from breakfast. He said, "What's up?"

We told him that we were to be guards at a court-martial. Then another guy came in and asked, "What are you gonna guard?"

"That was all the sergeant said," I told him.

Our uniforms did look good, and you could see yourself in our shoes. We always kept one pair of dress shoes ready, as well as a dress uniform.

Someone suggested we put our ponchos on to help keep the dampness from ruining the creases in our pants as well as our jackets. One of the boys had let us use his iron so we could get good creases, but in damp, rainy weather, it was all but impossible to keep our uniforms looking good.

We hurried from the barracks to the battery headquarters, trying not to step in any water that had pooled up. Our shoes did look good! And we stayed on the gravel walk to avoid the mud. As we walked into the building, a corporal who was sitting at a desk looked up from his stack of papers and said, "The first sergeant will be here in a few minutes. He is talking to the battery commander." Then he pointed toward an inner room, and said, "You'd better take off your ponchos and fold them up."

We stood and waited for what seemed like hours and

we watched the corporal count check marks on a roster that I felt sure had our names on it, but he didn't say anything.

The sergeant appeared holding a clipboard in his left hand. I am sure this included a list of what everybody in the battery would be doing today, or maybe even the whole week or even a month. He looked at us with a very critical eye, beginning with our haircuts and our shaves—which I didn't have to do very often, so I didn't think that was a problem. My beard was dark but thin and didn't grow very fast. I could tell he was looking at our jackets, then our pants and shoes. He asked us to turn around. "You men look OK," he said.

With dead seriousness, he said, "Let me tell you what this is all about. The first thing you will do is draw your weapons. You will have live ammunition. Do not put a live cartridge in the chamber. I do not have any idea that you will have to use your weapons, but you must be ready. The court-martial is in the recreation hall. MPs will bring the prisoner to court. We don't know anything about this person. He is from another unit. There will be an MP in the courtroom with you."

I wanted to ask why we needed live ammunition if there was going to be an MP in the room, but I knew not to interrupt.

"You two will be standing on each side of the door. You will stand at rest. When the officers come into the room, you will come to attention. The colonel will tell you, 'at ease.' I will bring you the live ammunition to put into your guns before the prisoner and the officers arrive. You are to say nothing unless the president of the court, our battalion commander, asks you a question. Usually there is no trouble, but under no condition do you let the prison escape. Shoot if you have to."

We followed the sergeant into the rec hall after we had gotten our weapons. It sure looked different from the last time I was there watching a couple of guys play ping-pong.

They were good. I had never seen anybody play ping-pong until I was in the army. I tried it several times, but I was not very good at it. The boys I played with had played before, and I hadn't. Maybe that was the problem.

All of a sudden, the sergeant called everyone to attention. There were only two other people in the hall besides the sergeant and the two of us guards. These, the sergeant told us, were clerks or messengers. We called them gofers. Then in walked the officers who were to hear the case. There was the colonel, two majors, a captain, and a lieutenant. The officers sat behind a table at the end of the room. Then two more officers came in—the prosecutor and the defense attorney. These officers were not lawyers, we found out, but they knew how to argue a case. They were good people and tried to be fair.

When all were present, the colonel said "at ease." In a few minutes, the outside door to the rec room, where we were standing—opened and the prisoner arrived between two tall MPs. But they weren't really so big. The prisoner, though, was massive. He must have weighed 250 pounds, and none of it was fat. I was only 5'8" tall, but this guy was at least a foot taller than I was. One of the MPs whispered something to the prisoner. That huge man stepped forward, and saluted the colonel. "Reporting as ordered, Sir." The colonel returned the salute and said, "Take your seat." He pointed to the chair next to the counsel for the prisoner.

As the colonel talked about the case, I listened carefully. It reminded me of when I had to go to court because I was accused of stealing and thought I would go to prison. I was sure scared then, and I guessed this prisoner, no matter how big he was, was scared too.

The colonel asked the prosecutor and defense if they were ready. They both said they were. He told the prosecutor to state his case. The prosecutor said that the prisoner had beat up people in a bar in a nearby town and caused $900 in damage to the place. He said the owner of the bar had called the police, who in turn had called the MPs. It sounded as if it took four policemen and two MPs to break up the fight. The owner of the bar pressed charges against the soldier.

The owner of the bar was the first witness. He told all about the fight and the damage to the bar. The defense counsel cross-examined the owner, and he admitted that he had not pressed charges against the four civilians even though they had been teasing the soldier. I guess they wouldn't have teased him very much if they had been able to see him stand up. He was probably sitting in a booth near the back of the bar where it was dark. He was by himself, too. If he had been with other soldiers, I don't think anyone would have teased him.

The defense tried to show that the soldier was provoked into fighting. The next witnesses were the police and the MPs. They said about the same thing that the owner had just said. This was the only evidence that the prosecutor had to offer.

Next the defense called the soldier to testify. He told the same story except he said that he told the civilians to leave him alone time and time again. The defense counsel asked him where he was from. He told him he was from Georgia. I don't remember the name of the town, but I do remember his accent. People always teased me about my Virginia accent. They laughed at the way I said "house" and "mouse," but this prisoner really had an accent. I loved to hear him talk. Maybe that had something to do with the fight. I could just picture these civilians asking him to say "fixin' to drink this pitcher of beer" again so they could laugh at him. The defense officer brought out that this fellow had only been in his unit a short time. He had no close friends but he had a good record. Both officers then gave their closing statements.

Then the colonel asked someone to get the MPs. They came and led the prisoner out. The defense and prosecuting officers also left the room.

The colonel looked around at the officers on the court and said, "Gentlemen, there doesn't seem to be any question about guilt. Every one agreed?"

Each officer was supposed to write "guilty" or "not guilty" on a piece of paper and put it in a hat that was passed around. The last person passed the hat back to the colonel. He took each piece out separately, unfolded it, and read what was on the paper. There were five officers making up the military court, and all five said the prisoner was guilty.

The colonel opened one of the books that he had brought with him and read the suggested punishment for being found guilty of assaulting a civilian and destroying civilian property. He read out the suggested punishment—six months at hard labor and forfeiture of all pay and allowances. The colonel said with a smile, "We will have to vote on this to make it legal. "Gentlemen, mark your ballots." As he wrote on his slip of paper, he said, "You can just put down six and six, and that will be OK."

The lieutenant on the end was writing a lot on his ballot. All the others had finished quickly, but the lieutenant even turned his paper over and continued to write on the back. Finally, he folded the paper and put it in the hat. The colonel took out one ballot at a time and read what was written. All the votes were for six and six except the last ballot which was the lieutenant's. The colonel took his time and read both sides of it.

When he had finished he jumped to his feet and said, "Who wrote this?" The lieutenant looked up and raised his hand and said, "I did, sir." Then the fireworks started. The colonel banged his fist on the table and said, "Lieutenant, I ordered you to vote six and six!"

The lieutenant looked the colonel straight in the eye and said slowly, "Sir, you can order me to do a lot of things, but you cannot order me how to vote."

I looked out of the corner of my eye at the other guard and saw him looking at me the same way. I looked at the table at the front of the room. I could hear rain hitting the windows outside, but inside, I couldn't hear a sound. I thought to myself, "This lieutenant has guts." But I wasn't sure they weren't going to get spilled all over the floor. The colonel said nothing. The other officers looked straight ahead as if they were in a daze. At last, the colonel sat down, but his face was as red as a beet. The lieutenant kept this eyes focused on the colonel. Slowly the colonel bowed his head and put one hand on his chin. Then he smiled.

He turned to the lieutenant and said, "Please tell me your reason for your vote, but before that, I want to read what you wrote on the ballot so the other officers will know what we are talking about. You said, "The punishment should be to fine the private one dollar and have him pay for the cost of one-fifth of the damage to the bar." I can't quite make out what the rest of this says." The colonel did not explain anything about the words he couldn't read. By now, the paper was balled up in his hand.

The lieutenant, still looking at the colonel, said, "We have all voted this man guilty of fighting in this bar and causing damage to the property; however, we, the army, have trained this man to fight. If we look again at his record, we can see that he is proficient at hand-to-hand combat. I think the army did a good job. It seems that he got the best of four people. The evidence shows that he did not start the fight and that he tried to keep from having to fight. But once he was committed to the fight, he did a good job. I don't think the army should encourage its people to fight in town, but we should not unduly punish our people for protecting themselves."

The room was silent. The colonel put his head back, with his hands behind his head and smiled. He said, "Gentlemen, I agree with the lieutenant. I think the private should pay a fine of one dollar and pay for one-fifth of the damage." The other officers quickly agreed, and the lieutenant looked relieved.

The prisoner was brought back in and the sentence was read to him from an official-looking paper the colonel had quickly filled out. The colonel said that the MPs would take the prisoner and a copy of the result of the court-martial back to the prisoner's unit. The prisoner couldn't stop smiling. He saluted the court, turned, and left the room. The colonel dismissed the court, went over to the lieutenant, and said as he put his hand on his shoulder, "Lieutenant, I think we should go to lunch together. It's my time to buy." The colonel and the lieutenant left, followed by the other officers.

As they walked past me, I heard one say to the other, "That lieutenant has guts."

The other officer replied, "Yes, and I think he was right."

"Well, the colonel thought he was right, and that's good enough for me."

A couple of weeks later I went on a three-day exercise as the driver for this lieutenant whose regular driver was in the hospital. We were attached to a headquarters. He ate with the officers, but he was always sure that I got my meals. The nights were clear and cool, but not cold. Most of us didn't mind sleeping outdoors if it wasn't raining, and the lieutenant and I were on an observation post most of the time. I had manned the radio while he observed what was supposed to be the front lines. Now here I was on an observation post observing an area occupied by a real enemy.

Sergeant Brown tapped me on the shoulder and whispered, "I'll take over for you now." When he asked if I had seen anything unusual. I said, "No." And then, keeping as close to the ground as I could, we slowly exchanged places.

Chapter Six

When I got to the back of the hill, I stretched. I wasn't stretching to shake sleepiness, but to get my circulation going in the cold, and it sure felt good. While manning the observation post, I had been covered with a blanket and a poncho, plus a field jacket, field pants, and long underwear. Also, I had been down in the foxhole, so the cold wind didn't feel like it was going right through me. Out there in the open it was cold.

It was still cloudy—low, big, dark clouds that seemed to be moving so fast, and it looked as if it were going to snow any minute.

Lieutenant Brown called to me softly from his foxhole. "Kid, don't you ever have to go to the bathroom?" Hesitating, I said, "I think I can now."

"Well," the voice said from the foxhole, "take your shovel and go, but don't dig too deep."

I hurried down the hill about thirty feet and found a soft spot of earth between two large rocks. I was right. I did have to, so I squatted and that was that. I used the toilet paper that we all carried in our pockets or in our helmet liners. As I filled up my shallow hole, I thought about the fact that I had never lived in a house with inside plumbing. Even at school,

33

we had outside johnny houses. My first real bathroom was in the barracks in the army. At home, I was used to washing in a basin or tub or even a bucket. My brother had talked about a shower, but I had never seen one until I was in the army.

The army bathroom was called the latrine. Along one wall were showers, about eight in a row. On another wall were a line of toilets with no partitions between them. What they called urinals were near the door. On the far side of the room were the basins or, as the sergeant called them, lavatories. It sure was nice to have all the water you wanted, especially hot water that you didn't have to heat on the stove. Just think. No one had to bring it in or carry it out after it was used.

One of the hardest things I had to get used to was going to the bathroom and taking a shower with a lot of other people. There was no privacy, but in the army, you can get used to almost anything.

As I returned to my foxhole to rest, the lieutenant asked me if I needed anything. That was really nice of him. I appreciated him asking, but I said, "No, thank you, sir." I didn't want to bother him.

Another thing that I appreciated was his language. I didn't like the language of the barracks. I had never heard people cuss in every sentence they spoke. My mother had always taught me not to take the Lord's name in vain. For years, I didn't know what that meant, but I finally understood it when I was in elementary school.

One of the boys was talking at recess and the teacher overheard his conversation and told him it was a poor way to express himself. She told us we would be better people if we did not cuss or take the Lord's name in vain. I always tried to do what she said, because it was what my mother had told me as well.

Even though my mother said that about the Lord, we didn't go to church. My mother said that she and my father used to go to church when they were first married, and they continued to go after my brother was born. It wasn't too long after that my father was taken sick. He died shortly after I was born. I couldn't remember him. I only remembered my mother talking about him, but still I felt as if I knew him.

Thinking about the language of the barracks, I remembered the morning that six of us got called to report after breakfast for sick call. I didn't know what was going on. This was in basic training. We had only been in the army a few weeks. And I wasn't sick.

Apparently everybody else knew what was going on except me, and we hurried to get in line for breakfast. After we were dismissed, several of the fellows made the same comment to me. They said, "So are you going to get it cut off this morning?" I still didn't know what they were talking about, and I never did find out until we got to the hospital that the army wanted me circumcised.

The doctor explained in detail and was very nice about it. He told us it was necessary to help us keep clean and to prevent diseases. He said, "The operation would not hurt."

I was the first in line to have it done. I was not used to getting undressed with nurses around, but I did what I was told. The doctor gave me several shots, which didn't hurt that much, and it was over in no time. From there, I went into a room with six beds that had a sign over the door that said "Recovery Room." I lay on the bed with a nightgown on me that tied in the back. One after the other, the boys came in when they were finished with their operations. They soon brought up lunch. It was a big meal and very good. About three hours after lunch the doctor came back into the recovery room and looked at each of us. He said we could go back to our unit.

Getting dressed was a little painful, but I was all right. All six of us had ridden to the hospital in the back of a 2 1/2 ton truck. Climbing into the truck for the ride back was very painful—but nothing like jumping out of the truck when we got back to our unit.

As we walked into the barracks, we saw pictures of naked women tacked up over our beds. The other fellows in the barracks were all talking about girls—their conquests and experiences, true or not, I didn't know. I asked the fellow in the bed next to mine what was going on. His name was Ray Stone. He looked at me with a smile on his face and said very shyly, "They are trying to get you to have an erection after your operation. I am sure you know it would be very painful."

What was I to do? I climbed on my bed, closed my eyes, and thought about home. In what seemed like just a few minutes, I felt someone pulling hard at my shoulder. I turned my head and opened one eye. It was the same fellow, Ray Stone. With that same smile he had earlier, he said, "It's time to go to the mess hall. You went to sleep. That's good." I guess I had gone to sleep.

This was the beginning of a friendship. Ray was from west Texas. He had been raised on a ranch by his father and older sister. He was tall and thin with sandy hair, a good-looking boy until he opened his mouth. Parts of his front teeth looked like they were worn away, and they weren't all the same color. Later Ray told me his tooth problem was caused by too much fluoride. I didn't know what this meant, and I don't think Ray did either.

He and I were later to go to motor school together. This was where they taught us to drive and to care for our vehicles. After motor school, Ray got orders to go to Europe. My orders were to go to Fort Lewis, Washington, which meant on to Korea. We promised each other that we would write, but I never heard from him, nor did I ever write to him.

During those weeks in basic training and motor school together, we talked about what we were going to do when we got out of the army. I told him about my idea of going to a trade school under the GI Bill. He thought that would be good, although he said he had no interest in going to school anymore. He had finished high school and the only things he talked about were going back and working on his father's ranch and marrying a girl named Sue whom he had known since the first grade. He used to say, "She has red hair and teeth like mine. I wonder what our children will look like."

Thinking about Ray Stone reminds me of the first Christmas I was in the army. We were told we could apply for leave at Christmas. Some would get leave at Christmas; others at New Year's. I thought going home would be great, but each month I sent all but $10.00 home to my mother by money order. The $10.00 was to pay for my haircuts, cleaning, movies, and trips to the PX. Also, they took out an allotment from my pay for her. I knew that my brother and his wife were trying to help my mother, too. There was no way she could get by on the allotment and what little I could send her. In her letters, she never complained, but I knew things were tight.

Ray asked me to go home with him to Texas for Christmas. He told me the bus ride wouldn't cost much and we could stay at his house. We would be gone seven days. Ray even asked his sister if it was all right if he brought me home with him for the holiday. His sister wrote to me and asked me to come, but I told Ray I was going to save my money and try to go home after motor school.

Even the first sergeant called me aside one morning and asked me if I was applying for leave for the holiday. When I told him I wasn't, he asked why. I told him about my mother and about what I did with my money. He turned his head away from me. When he turned back, he said, "I'll be glad to loan you the money to go home." I thanked him, but I just didn't want to owe money.

Chapter Seven

The main reason I decided not to go home with Ray for Christmas was that after I finished driver training early in the new year, I felt sure they would give me leave. All of us felt we would go to Korea, although we had heard that some might go to Europe. Wherever I went, I had to get home first. My plan was to save all the money I could— which wasn't much. I went to the bus station on post to check the cost of a ticket home. The army gave us travel pay based on going by railroad. I hadn't even checked the railroad cost because I knew going by bus would be cheaper.

The week before Christmas was cloudy and cold, but everybody had a smile on their face, mostly because they knew they were going home. Most of the boys in my barracks had gotten leave for Christmas. The rest would have leave at New Year's. Christmas Day was on Sunday. On Friday, they told us there would be no duty on Saturday. Some of those going home for leave left Thursday night. The rest left Friday morning before formation. Only about five boys were left in my barracks, and I didn't know any of them well. I knew their names, but I had not had much to do with any of them.

In the morning formation, there were about half as many

present as usual. After the report, when the first sergeant had taken charge of our battery, we were given instructions and duties for the day. It was just busy work, and he told us there would be no formation on Saturday and, of course, none on Sunday.

So what I did on Friday was such things as shine my shoes, help clean up the barracks, and—generally, nothing. I even took a nap after writing to my mother, but I didn't miss a meal. That night I went to a movie. *White Christmas* was showing. I enjoyed the movie, but it made me feel homesick.

Saturday morning I slept late. I didn't get up until 7:15 A.M. which was three hours later than usual. After dressing, I hurried to the mess hall. To my surprise, there were only half a dozen people eating.

I finished my breakfast, and then I went back to the barracks. There was no one left on my floor. I lived on the first floor and had very seldom gone upstairs. The boys who lived upstairs were in my same battery, and I knew some of them fairly well, but I hadn't seen anyone that I knew well at breakfast.

As I climbed the stairs, I counted half a dozen people still in bed. I guess they had a party the night before, but I sure hadn't heard anybody come in late or make a lot of noise.

About 10:00 A.M., I decided I would go to the main PX on post. It was probably a mile and a half walk. I had only been there twice and hadn't bought anything either time. I decided not to get a bus. That time of day, the wait could have been an hour or more.

Walking along the edge of the hard-surface road, the cold, damp wind hit me in the face. The temperature was probably in the high thirties. The sun peeked through the broken clouds overhead, but off to the west, there was a large, dark bank of clouds. It looked like a thunderstorm coming, but I couldn't believe that. Back home in Virginia, we usually had thunderstorms only in the summertime.

Anyway, I thought I could get to the PX before it rained if it was going to. In my short time at Fort Sill in Oklahoma, I had learned the weather could change quickly. It seemed one minute there was a warm breeze coming from the south, and the next minute the wind was blowing hard and cold from the north. I had heard one of the sergeants say that if you didn't like the Oklahoma weather, you should wait a minute. It would change.

As I walked along the road, I thought about my Christmas at home. We never had many gifts, but I loved my mother, and I knew she loved me. The worst thing about Christmas was going back to school after the holiday. The kids would all stand up in class and tell what they had gotten for Christmas. When my turn came, I would say that all I got was clothes. I remember one boy said—kind of under his breath, but I could hear him—that if I got all these clothes, why didn't I ever wear any of them to school. I wanted to punch him in the nose, but I didn't. Instead, I decided not to go to school the rest of the week. By the next week everybody had forgotten all about Christmas.

As I got close to the PX, I decided I would look for a present for my mother. I could leave it in my locker until my driver training was over. I was sure I would get leave then. There was no use mailing it. Christmas was the next day, and I wanted to see the expression on her face when she opened my package.

At home, I always made all of the presents I gave her at Christmas. One time I carved a bird out of a knot of a wild cherry tree. Another time, I tied corn shucks together to make a doormat. It wasn't good and soon fell apart, but she had praised it anyway. Then there was the time I took oyster shells, washed them real good, cut a hole in each one, and ran a string through them. This decoration, I told her, was for our Christmas tree, and she always put it on the tree, even though the shells slipped and had to be rearranged. As

I pulled open the door to enter the PX, I was wondering if she had hung my shells this year.

The PX didn't look like it did the last time I was in there. The center aisle had a Christmas tree with many decorations on it, including electric lights of various colors, and under the tree, there were packages all wrapped up in different colored paper. It sure was a sight to see.

Almost nobody was in the store, other than clerks. Most army people had probably gone home on leave—after all, this was Christmas Eve. There was a sign on each cash register that said the PX would close at 3:00 P.M. on Christmas Eve and would be closed all day on Christmas so that employees could be home with their families.

As I walked up and down the aisles, several clerks asked if they could help me, but I didn't want any help. I said I was just looking. When I came upon a rack of jackets, I asked a sales clerk if they were for men or women. She said, "Either." She asked me what size I wanted. She had a very pleasant smile and a kind voice. I told her I was looking for a jacket for my mother for Christmas, but I didn't know what size she wore. She asked me with that nice smile if my mother was tall or short, large or small. I looked at her from head to toe and told her that my mother was about her size. She told me that this jacket didn't fit tight, that you wore it over other clothes. She offered to try one on if I would just pick out a color. I picked a bluish gray one. She said, "That's my favorite color, too."

I didn't know whether she was sincere or if she was pulling my leg to make a sale. As she removed the jacket from the hanger, I asked her how long she had been working there. She said, "Just a week." She had started college in September and she said she needed to make money during the holiday to help pay her way toward the second semester. She also told me that she had worked in the PX during the summer. A neighbor of hers was a manager and had gotten her the job. She asked me where I was from. I said,

"Virginia." She said she had talked to people from Virginia before, but they didn't have the same accent I did.

She looked good in the jacket. She wanted to know if I liked it. I told her I did, but I thought to myself that I wasn't sure whether it was the jacket or her I liked better.

"Well," she said, "are you going to buy it? If you are, I will wrap it for you." I told her I would take it. Then she told me the price.

I was shocked. "There goes my savings for the bus trip home on leave," I thought. Maybe I could hitch a ride.

Anyway I knew my mother would enjoy that jacket, and I had enjoyed talking to the nice girl.

It didn't take her long to wrap the package. I paid her and left with it.

Chapter Eight

I carried my package under my arm as I went out the door of the PX. I was sure proud, but I wasn't sure what made me the happiest—buying a present for my mother, or meeting a nice girl.

Immediately, I began trying to figure out a way to see this girl again, but I knew there wasn't anything I could do until after Christmas. On my way home, the wind picked up and it got real misty. When I looked up at the sky, I could see dark clouds. They looked like they were rolling over each other in the northwest. I was thinking it was certainly going to snow when several wet snowflakes landed on my glasses.

I looked around for a bus and luckily, one was just coming by, I hopped on it. I really wasn't sure where the bus was going, but I knew it would eventually get close to my unit headquarters. Also, I had no where to be, and no assigned duties, so I thought I might as well enjoy the ride.

For field exercises I always rode in the back of a truck with canvas over it, and could only see out of the back. The bus gave me a chance to really see Fort Sill. Off in the distance, I could see the mountains in Medicine Park. I couldn't see the tops because of the low clouds, but on the bus I could see the big rocks sticking out of winter grass. I knew there was a herd of buffalo in the park, but I had never seen it. I thought maybe one day one of the boys who had a car would ride up there and take me. I really wanted to see the buffalo. I had heard some of the boys in the barracks talk about going up there. They said there were about fifty buffalo that were real tame, meaning you could get close to them. Also, they said the view from the top of the mountain at Medicine Park was fabulous. They said on a clear day, you could see for miles and you could see the buffalo grazing. You could see all of Fort Sill and Lawton, the town nearby. They said there were wheat fields to the north and west. This time of year, everything would look brown I guessed, but in the spring the green fields and grasslands would be pretty.

What I didn't see, almost anywhere, were trees. The trees I did see were small and didn't have any leaves. In eastern Virginia we had trees that lost their leaves, but we also had pine trees that stayed green all the time.

Here in Oklahoma, most of the land was without trees. Only along dry creek beds did you see any trees. I didn't know why they were called creek beds, because I had sure never seen any water in them. But someone told me that sometimes there were flash floods, and then the water would rise very fast.

I thought about the girl in the PX again. I wondered what she was going to do that night. Maybe I could call her, I thought. But I didn't even know her name.

We passed a rifle range. I wasn't sure if this was the same one I had been on, but it was similar. I remembered the sergeant in class telling us how to hold our weapon, squeeze the trigger, and position it on our shoulder with a sling. I tried to picture the sergeant but saw the face of the girl in the PX instead.

I tried to remember all the instructions they gave us about caring for our weapons, primarily about cleaning them.

I'll never forget the sergeant screaming, "Never aim the weapon at anything you don't want to shoot and never shoot anything you don't want to kill!" I wondered if the blonde girl from the PX had ever had to learn to shoot.

The officer in charge of our group was very good. He gave commands that were clear and direct. He helped me personally and after I shot at targets he gave me the results. I did really well, and I thought I could show them to the nice girl in the PX with the blue eyes and blonde hair. I didn't even know her name.

We were given a clip of five cartridges and told when to load. They said not to fire until we heard the command. We were to fire at our own speed and at our assigned target. The command came: "The flag is up. The flag is waving. The flag is down. Commence firing." Some of the boys got their five shots off quickly. I tried to shoot slowly and to squeeze the trigger as I had been told. I had never shot a gun until I was in the army. I just wanted to hit my target. When I finished my five shots, the officer shouted, "Cease fire." A couple of shots went off close to me after the cease-fire order was given. I heard some of the sergeants holler at the boys who shot late. I think they got the point quickly. I sure would have.

Our group had been divided up before rifle practice. Some boys were in the pits beneath the targets. These targets could be raised and lowered. After a shot, the sergeant would ask the person in charge of the target for a signal about the accuracy of the shot. A complete miss was a signal called "Maggie's drawers." I never knew what this meant, but it always brought a laugh. We were all nervous about the results of our shots. I couldn't believe how bad some of the shots were. One boy close to me shot and hit the target next to his. Another person missed his target on all but one shot.

When my results came, I was surprised. There were three bulls eyes and two near bulls eyes. The sergeant asked me who had taught me to shoot. He was all smiles when I told him he had.

It felt good to hear all the boys around me telling me how well I shot. I was surprised and pleased.

I was thinking about telling the girl about my shooting skills, when the bus driver asked me what unit I was in. I told him, "The next stop will be close." Then I told him I didn't have anything to do, so I wanted to ride around the post. He said, "Fine." After the next stop, I was the only person on the bus. I moved forward when the driver started talking to me, asking me where I was from and if I was going home for New Year's. It was obvious I was not going to Virginia for Christmas as it was already Christmas Eve. I told him I hoped to go after I finished the driver-training course. He told me they would give me leave before my next assignment. The bus driver seemed like a very nice man, and he told me about his experiences in the army during World War II as we rode along.

We passed a lot of firing ranges for different types of weapons, most of which I didn't know anything about. We also passed the building where gas training was held. I remembered that well. They had taken us inside in small groups with an instructing officer. The officer instructed us on how to put on a gas mask. Then we did it ourselves and were checked by the officer.

Then he told us to take off our masks. The officer opened a container of tear gas, or something, and as soon as it started out into the room, he gave the order to put on our gas masks. After a few minutes, we were marched out of a door and told to remove our masks. You could still smell the stuff in our clothes, and our eyes watered, but we recovered outdoors. I wondered if that girl had ever experienced anything like that. I didn't think so, so that was something else I could tell her.

It wasn't too long before the bus got to my unit, I thanked the bus driver, and he wished me a "Merry Christmas." I also wished him and his family a "Merry Christmas," too. Then I remembered that he hadn't mentioned a family. Maybe I said the wrong thing.

As I walked toward my barracks, I noticed the wind had changed. It was from the south and was warmer than when I had walked to the PX earlier in the morning. The sky was still cloudy, but it was different: more overcast with lower clouds. As I went into my barracks, I didn't see anyone. I put the package for my mother in my foot locker and checked the lock several times after I locked it. Then I decided to lie across my bed until it was time to go to the mess hall for supper.

Across the room was a clothes locker where one of the boys kept a radio. He usually hung it on the handle of the locker with a piece of twine during the evening, but he put it in the locker during inspection and while we were on duty. I thought he may have put it in his foot locker this time. It was all right not having a radio though. I had a song singing itself in my head. It was "There's No Place Like Home For the Holidays."

When I thought it was about time for supper, I went to the mess hall. There was no line so I went in. There were two people on KP that I didn't know, and one cook I hadn't ever seen before. As I looked around some more, I saw boys eating that I hadn't seen before. As I held my tray out for the food, I heard one cook say to the other, "These boys had better eat good tonight because they won't get much tomorrow." This puzzled me at the time.

After I got my tray full, I realized I was hungry. I went to one of the tables where the boys were eating. We had been told that all tables were to be filled as people came in. No saving seats for your friends is what the mess sergeant had said. I asked one of the boys if he was new to the unit. He laughed and said, "No." They closed two of the other mess halls because most of the people are on leave. But the food sure is good here."

I told him that it was and there was plenty of it. We later talked about where we were from and what we were doing on Christmas Day. He said he and several others from his unit were invited to dinner in town at the home of one of the married boys in his unit. As we ate, we talked more, and we finally decided to go to a movie that night on post. It was the same movie I had seen the night before—*White Christmas*—but it was something to do, and Robert, who was from West Virginia, seemed like a nice fellow.

After returning from the movie, I decided to check out the radio that was supposed to be in the clothes locker across the barracks. I found the locker unlocked. Slowly, I opened the door and there on the floor of the locker was the radio. I didn't hesitate to move it to my clothes locker behind my bed and tie it to the handle. Neal Flynn from Mississippi, its owner, had told all of us to play it anytime we wanted, just not too loud so the sergeant wouldn't ban it from the barracks. He had told us that it ran on batteries and that the batteries lasted a long time. Neal had been to college three years, but he was drafted like I was.

Anyway, that night I was just lying in bed listening to the radio and thinking. The announcer kept talking about Christmas and it made me sad. I missed being home, more than I would have thought. I guessed I was homesick, and I thought maybe I could tell that to the girl in the PX, too.

Chapter Nine

Sleep finally came. When I opened my eyes, I thought it was light outside. I looked around. The lights were shining through the open latrine door. Also the light over the outside door was on, and all the beds were empty. For a moment I wondered if I was dreaming or awake.

Suddenly, I remembered where I was and why I was alone. I was in Oklahoma in the army, and this was Christmas Day. This was my first Christmas away from home. I missed home, and I missed my mother. There was nothing to get up for, and there was nothing to do. So I snuggled back under the covers. I wondered what the PX blonde was doing. I thought maybe tomorrow I would go to the PX.

All of a sudden, I felt hungry. I didn't think it was past breakfast, but I thought I better go eat. It was no use to miss a meal, even if I did expect a big Christmas dinner. At Thanksgiving, the mess hall had really put on a show. What was it they said? Turkey with all the trimmings! Well, whatever they called it, it was good!

I got out of bed and dressed quickly. It was so cold without any heat on in the barracks. I put on my field jacket as I rushed out of the door. It was cloudy and the wind was blowing. I thought maybe it would snow, but maybe not. It would probably rain.

At home I didn't like snow or rain. It made getting in wood too hard. No one dumped a nice pile of wood in our back yard. I had to go into the woods and cut down dead trees. Then I cut them up with my ax and carried them to the house. It seemed I could never get ahead on my wood chores. If it was raining or there was snow on the ground, my gloves were always wet and then the ax could slip.

I didn't see anyone moving about as I was hurrying to the mess hall, and when I got there I rushed to open the door. The door was locked! I couldn't believe it. I put my head against the window and looked in. There was no one there, nor were there any lights on except the exit lights. I thought at first maybe another mess hall was open, but then I remembered the other boys coming to this mess hall because they said their mess halls were closed. It took me a minute, but I realized there would be no breakfast. I remembered the mess sergeant saying we had better eat well. Now I knew what he was talking about.

I turned around and walked back to my barracks. I thought about the boy, Robert, I had gone to the movie with the night before. He had said several of them were going to a married friend's house in town for breakfast and to watch a football game on TV. Then they were going to stay for Christmas dinner. I sure wished I had a married friend.

Back in the barracks, I realized why there was no heat. The fireman had probably been asked out to eat too.

I turned on the radio and listened to Christmas music, then I read the last letters from my mother. I was too lonesome and hungry, so I finally went to sleep.

When I woke up, it was even colder than before. I had taken off my shoes and pulled the cover over me, but I had not undressed. The announcer gave the time on the radio. It was 1:00. I decided I would go to the PX—not the main PX, but a PX nearby. You could buy candy, pop, beer, popcorn, and hot dogs there. I didn't drink beer, but I thought a hot dog or two would be good. On the half mile walk there, I saw several boys going in and out of barracks on my way. It was nice knowing I was not the only person on post.

Near the PX, I looked for signs of activity, but I didn't see anyone or anything. There were no lights on inside the building. My heart sank, until I noticed a sign on the door. It was very clear: "Open at 6 P.M. Christmas Day." It was now 2:00 P.M.

Walking back to the barracks, I looked up at the clouds. The sky was clearing, and I thought maybe the sun would shine. My mother always said things were better if the sun was shining, and right then I sure agreed with her. I began to think there was even a chance the mess hall would open for dinner.

As I climbed the steps going into the barracks, I could see my shadow. Everything seemed better. I had been hungry many times before, so I knew I could wait for 6:00 P.M. And if the mess hall was open, I wouldn't have to spend my money on hot dogs.

That afternoon I sat on my bed and wrote a letter to my mother. Maybe it was wrong, but I described Thanksgiving dinner as if it were Christmas dinner. I told her about the turkey, dressing, cranberry sauce, and pumpkin pie. I told her about going to see the movie *White Christmas* and asked a lot of questions about what she was doing and how she was making out living in North Carolina. Did she like it? Were the people friendly? I went on and on.

When it was time to eat, I went to the mess hall, but it was still closed, so I started out for the PX. I could just taste the hot dogs, with mustard, and a bottle of pop would wash it all down. I didn't care what kind. I was on the doorstep at 5:30. Promptly at 6:00 P.M., two men and a lady came and opened the door. I rushed in behind them. The lady asked me what my hurry was. I told her I hadn't eaten all day. As she listened, her eyes watered a little.

"I'll take care of you," she said.

She went to the refrigerator and took out three hot dogs and put them in a small pan with water on a gas stove. She also heated the rolls in a toaster and asked me what I wanted to drink.

"Pepsi is fine," I said.

It didn't take long for me to eat the hot dogs and drink the Pepsi. I went to pay the lady, and asked her how much. She looked me straight in the eye and said, "Nothing, son. It's Christmas."

I thanked her several times and noticed a tear on her cheek as she turned away from me. I thought maybe she had been hungry before, too.

Back in the barracks, it was too quiet and I didn't have anything to do, so I decided to go to a movie. There was still no heat, and I didn't want to go to bed that early. I had already slept part of the morning, so I spent another quarter and saw *White Christmas* for the third time. I also spent a dime for a big bag of popcorn. It stopped me from burping and tasting those hot dogs.

I walked back to the barracks from the movie theater. The moon was out, and the stars looked so bright. I hoped tomorrow would be a better day. Also I was sure there wouldn't be much work to do and I could go back to the main PX and see the college girl.

Sleep came easily that night. I left the radio on very softly, and during the night, I was conscious of people coming into the barracks. I think some were coming back from leave early. Maybe some had just been visiting in town. Everyone with a pass was supposed to be in formation at 6:30. People who went AWOL were not treated very well, no matter the excuse.

After breakfast the next morning when the duties were announced, I had almost nothing to do. I asked the sergeant in charge of my detail if I could go to the main PX.

He said, "Okay, but don't stay too long."

I walked toward the main PX, thinking it was no use

wasting time waiting for a bus. The weather was clear, and the wind was blowing, but it was a warm wind coming from the southwest. In the PX, I started for the aisle where I had bought the jacket for my mother. I was shocked to see a sign over the jacket rack that said, "Half price sale." I stood dumbfounded. I had spent most of the money I had saved for three months on that jacket, and now it would cost half of what I had paid.

I came back to my senses when the salesperson, the college girl who had sold me the jacket, said, "Excuse me. Can I help you?" I just shook my head.

She said, "How did your mother like her jacket?"

I replied that it was in my foot locker.

She said, "Oh, that's right. You're from Virginia."

I told her it didn't seem right that I paid full price for the jacket on Saturday and on Monday it was half price.

She said, "We didn't sell very many, and we're having a sale." She told me she didn't know on Saturday that the jackets would be on sale on Monday. The manager had told her that morning to put up a half-price-sale sign.

I told her about saving my money to go home. I said how I wanted to take my mother a present.

She looked at me with a twinkle in her eye and said, "Have you opened the package since I wrapped it?"

"No," I said.

Then she said, "Do you have the sales slip?"

I told her I didn't know what a sales slip was, but I had a receipt that she had given me.

She smiled, "Give me this slip and go get the package, and I will work something out."

I told her I didn't want to get her in trouble with the boss. I knew she needed the job. I just stood there.

She just looked at me and said, "Go."

Still I stood there looking at her pretty smile.

She kept smiling and saying, "Go get the package."

I ran back to the barracks, opened my foot locker, and

got the package that was still all neatly tied up with Christmas wrapping paper. Double time, I rushed back to the PX. No sooner had I gotten in the door, than I saw the blonde girl wave at me. I rushed over to her, and she took the package from me, almost pulling it away. There were almost no customers that day, and all the sales people were counting things on the shelves and racks, and in the showcases. She told me to wait there.

It seemed like a long wait, but it couldn't have been over five minutes. I stood there, trying not to be in the way, but several clerks asked if they could help me. I thanked them and said no, that I was being helped. Then to my surprise, I saw the smiling blonde girl coming toward me with a package that seemed to be the same one she had taken from me.

"What's up?" I asked.

"I got another jacket just about the same color, and here is half of what you paid." She put the money in my hand and folded my fingers over the crisp bills and change. I thanked her, and then, to my own surprise, I asked her if I could see her one evening after work. She said yes, but that the next couple of days and evenings she would be taking inventory.

We agreed on Thursday evening. I would meet her at 6:30 at the PX, and we would go to a movie on post. Then I would ride home with her on a bus. For the first time, I noticed her name tag.

"See you Thursday, Pamela Hill," I said. I was whistling when I left the PX.

Chapter Ten

Pamela Hill was as far away now as Virginia or my mother in North Carolina. I was in a foxhole on the backside of Hill 4413, and it was colder than the barracks that Christmas at Fort Sill.

I raised up to see who was in the foxhole next to me. It was Lieutenant Brown. The clouds were large and dark and moving from left to right across the sky. I had asked Sergeant Kelly once why the clouds seemed to move that way. He said the weather this time of year came from Russia and was probably heading to the Pacific Ocean. Next to me, the lieutenant snored softly. He was a big man. Curled up, with all of his clothes on, in a foxhole, he looked even larger.

All of a sudden there was the loud whining of shells going over my head. I didn't know where they were headed, so I leaned over and tapped on the lieutenant's shoulder. He was awake instantly. He listened for a few seconds and said, "These shells are incoming." He said he would change places with Sergeant Kelly so he could look through the telescope.

"What are you going to look for?"

"I want to see if I can tell where the shells are being fired from." I didn't know what difference this would make, but I knew he thought it was important. The shells kept coming, and we could hear them exploding not far to our rear. After what seemed an eternity of silence Sergeant Kelly scrambled over the hill and into the foxhole. He told me the guns we heard firing were probably in a gully behind the hills to our front. He said he and the lieutenant were trying to see if they could see smoke where the guns were firing.

He explained that if you could locate the direction the firing was coming from and figure where the shells were landing, you could plot these points on a map and get the approximate locations of the gun emplacements. Sergeant Kelly said the forward observers would send any information they had to the fire control center. I reminded him that we couldn't break radio silence unless there was an attack. He said, "We won't use the radio, but we'll have the information to send back in case of an attack."

The shelling began again and continued for about half an hour. It stopped just as suddenly as it had started. Everything seemed still. There was not a sound to be heard, and I wondered if the shells had hit the unit we passed through or if some of them had landed farther to the rear, near our artillery. I asked the sergeant what he thought would happen now. He said it was hard to tell. Our artillery might begin firing any time, or they might wait until later. The enemy might begin firing again, he said.

I began to think. If there were forward observers on both sides, as we had been told, why were we here? Any attack that was coming could certainly be reported by them. I asked the sergeant this question. Our foxholes were real close, and we could talk softly so no one could hear. I was sure even the lieutenant couldn't hear us. We were too far down the hill.

The sergeant joked, "You don't know the army. Our unit wants this extra observation post probably because if the forward observers get hit in the initial attack, we could get the information to our units in the rear. Our forward observer positions are probably known to the enemy. Do you remember me telling you how we trace the shell fired from an artillery battery? The enemy does the same thing. They learn the direction our shells are fired and any corrections made by the forward observers, and trace it on a map."

This made a little sense to me. The sergeant gave me the idea that the army had a plan. It made me feel better to know our mission served a purpose.

Suddenly, there were a terrific number of enemy shells coming in over our heads. We could hear them whine through the air, and it seemed they would never end. The explosions to our rear covered a large area. Then the shelling stopped as abruptly as it had started. I asked the sergeant if he thought our units to the rear had been hit. I told him I had seen those shells exploding over a huge area.

He said, "If you had any sense, you would keep your head down in the foxhole. You can look after the attack is over." He thought I was crazy to watch the shells explode as if they were fireworks, but I was glad the sergeant told me what to do.

I looked all around at the sky. The clouds were rolling in again, and the wind was picking up. It was still damp, and I thought maybe it would snow again.

Again, we began to hear the whining of shells going over our heads. This time they came from the opposite direction. This meant that our artillery was firing at the enemy. The explosions seemed to be not far away, somewhere over on the other side of the hill. I don't know exactly, but they were so close you could feel the ground shake. Sergeant Kelly cautioned me again to lay low just as another of the shells exploded near the crest of the hill to our front. Then all was quiet again for a few moments, and I raised up to look around.

About that time, there was a terrific explosion and my side felt like it was on fire. This time, there had been no whining to warn us. The shell hadn't gone over our heads. It had come from our own guns, and I was hit. I was afraid to look. I moved my right hand down near my waist. I felt a hole in my jacket. My hand felt warm. I pulled my hand out of the jacket hole so I could see it. It was red with blood.

"Sergeant, I'm hit."

"Is it bad?" he asked.

"I don't think so, but I'm bleeding." I asked him if he was okay. He said, yes, and he told me to stay down. He said to take out my first aid kit pack and put pressure on the bleeding with the large compress gauze.

There was no more shelling, but we waited for what seemed like hours to be sure. I think I must have gone to sleep, because I was awakened by Sergeant Kelly at the edge of my foxhole. He wanted to know how I was doing. I was still holding the bandage over the wound, and I said, "I think I am doing okay." He asked if I had one wound or several. I told him I didn't know. The truth is, I was afraid to look.

He told me that when he had tried to call me, I hadn't answered, so he had crawled to the edge of my foxhole. He told me to turn on my side the best I could and to keep holding pressure on the wound. He said he didn't see any other place I had been hit, but as I turned, I could feel a warmth going to my back. The pressure was not stopping the bleeding.

He leaned farther over my foxhole and said he was going to cut away my clothes to see the wound better. I said okay. The blood was still going toward my back, and I knew I was bleeding a lot. I just hoped the gauze could stop it.

After he had cut away my clothes, he put the compress gauze from his first aid kit on the wound. He told me to keep still and to hold the pack with firm but steady pressure. I said I was thirsty.

Sergeant Kelly's face grew pale. I wondered why. Then I remembered that in first aid classes in basic training we had been told not to give people a drink if there was a wound to the gut. His reaction told me the wound could be serious. I might be bleeding on the inside. Is this why the bleeding wouldn't stop? Is this why I was thirsty? I knew we couldn't leave this observation post, and I wondered if this meant I would bleed to death?

Sergeant Kelly told me to stay still and keep the pressure on the wound. He said he would tell Lieutenant Brown about me and see what we could do. Before he left me, he put the blanket that had fallen on the floor of the foxhole over me. One edge was wet with blood, and I smelled urine.

"This won't do," the sergeant said. He crawled to his foxhole and came back with his blanket. He threw my blanket up on the side of the foxhole and wrapped his blanket over me in two layers. He said he would come back soon.

I heard him crawling away, then his movement became faint. Then I heard nothing. I wondered what he was going to tell the lieutenant. What was going to happen to me? Luckily, I dozed off.

Chapter Eleven

I wondered what category of wounded they would put me in. In basic training, I learned there were three classes of wounded: Those who would get better if you didn't do anything; those who would live if they received treatment; and those who would die anyway.

I remembered that we were not to leave our post until we were relieved or attacked. Would I be left here if we were attacked? How would they move me? I knew I couldn't walk. I was too weak, and I was still bleeding, and I was so thirsty. There was no way I could reach my canteen, but maybe that was for the best. Sergeant Kelly and Lieutenant Brown were good men, and I knew they would do the best they could for me.

After a while, I opened my eyes and looked up at the sky. I was definitely conscious. I could see an occasional snowflake, but it was warm under the sergeant's blanket. Both of my hands felt numb from pressing on the bandage, but I kept pressing anyway.

I thought about home in the summertime. I was walking in the grassy lane with my childhood friend, Jay. We had our dogs with us—Prince and Lollipop, and we were on the way to Mr. Howe's landing. He let me use his skiff. We would probably crab around the shore or maybe go for a swim—although neither of us could swim too good. The water was not very deep. In most places we could jump off the boat and touch bottom. Then we would dog paddle around and climb back into the boat. The fact that we didn't have bathing suits was never a problem. There was no house anywhere around, and there was never anyone who could see us.

Mr. Howe always came back late in the afternoon after he had fished his crab pots and sold his crabs. He used to get gas and bait on the way home. I knew his routine, and I would go with him on occasion. He always wanted to pay me for helping him on the boat. He had a hard time getting around as he had only one leg, so when I went with him, he gave me a dollar.

One time I asked him how he had lost his leg. He said three winters before it had felt numb and was red and swollen. Dr. Llewellyn suggested he better go to the public health hospital in Baltimore. There he had been diagnosed with circulation problems. He was advised that standing in the boat all day was bad for his legs. He said he couldn't see what was ahead of him while steering the boat if he sat down, so he kept standing up. He didn't take the medicine regularly that they gave him, and I knew he hadn't been able to afford to pay someone to help him on the boat regularly.

I went to see Mr. Howe last winter, after he came home from the hospital, having had his leg amputated and an artificial leg made. He seemed to be getting around the house pretty well, but I didn't see how he was going to work his crabpots when it was rough. He told me he had always worked on the water, and had done some house painting in the off season. He wouldn't be able to climb a ladder any more, so he would have to continue crabbing.

"I have a wife and child to support, and crabbing is all I can do," he said. "My father was in an accident while working in a menhaden fish processing plant, and walked with a crutch the rest of his life. He raised a few watermelons and cantaloupes to sell to make a little money."

Mr. Howe knew how it was growing up poor. He wanted to help me by giving me a little work, even though he didn't make much money, and he let me use his skiff to catch soft crabs around the shore.

As soon as the dock came into view that summer day, we hurried to the skiff, calling our dogs as we ran. We had no oars, but I picked up a crab net. This was a long pole with a metal loop and net at one end. This was used to pick up soft crabs. Jay grabbed a board that had been shaped like a paddle. It was a sight to remember: two boys and two dogs in a half-sunken boat about twelve feet long. The one with the net stood on the bow; the other was in the stern trying to keep the dogs still so they wouldn't rock the boat.

When we arrived at the dock, we didn't notice that the tide was high. High tide was not a good time to look for soft crabs because you couldn't see them when the water was deep at the shoreline. When we noticed the tide was high and rising, we decided that crabbing was hopeless that afternoon.

Even today, that afternoon is still one of my best memories. I think of it as "the invasion." As a child growing up during World War II, I noticed the news seemed to be all about invasions—the invasion of North Africa, the invasion of Italy, the invasion of the many Pacific islands. Well, this local invasion was different.

On the farm opposite where Mr. Howe lived, Dr. Llewellyn, had gotten some goats to eat his briars and honeysuckle. However, the goats got out and eventually wound up in the woods behind Mr. Howe's, living on the plants and leaves they could reach by standing on their hind legs. The goats had been there about two years.

We decided we would invade the point of land and find the goats. As we approached, we could see maybe ten goats—nannies, billies, and their kids—sunning themselves on a bare spot of ground on the highest point of land. We made our plans. One of us would use the homemade paddle. The other would paddle with the crab net. We would get the dogs to bark and as soon as we came ashore, we would run up the bank and scare the goats into running.

Our plan went well at first. We ran up the bank, slipping and sliding in the loose sand and gravel. The dogs were beside us barking and sure enough, the goats ran back into the woods. But then, all of a sudden, the goats turned and ran after the dogs and us. We turned and hustled down the bank, the dogs on our heels with the goats not far behind. We pushed the boat off the shore, the dogs jumped in, and we shoved off. The goats came only as far as the water's edge, never making a sound. Our dogs were as quiet as mice, sitting as close to us as they could in the boat. We looked at each other and began to laugh as we drifted farther from shore and farther from the goats.

Lieutenant Brown tapped me on my shoulder. He asked how I was. I told him I felt okay, but that my hands were numb. He leaned over the edge of the foxhole and removed the sergeant's blanket. He told me to lift my hands up. I knew he was raising up the compress. I could feel the blood run down the side of my leg. The lieutenant made no comment as he placed the bandages back over the wound and placed my hands over the bandages. He pulled the blanket over me and put his poncho over the blanket. He told me it would keep me warmer. I couldn't remember what had happened to my poncho. I thought it was under me as we usually carried them in our belts, hanging down over our butts.

I couldn't wait any longer. I wanted to know what the lieutenant thought about my wounds, but I couldn't think of how to ask him. After all, he was an officer. But finally, I said, "What do I do, lieutenant?"

His reply was quick. "I don't know how deep your wound is, but the fragment probably came out of your back, and I don't want to turn you over. Lying on your back may be keeping the wound from bleeding. Don't take any liquid or eat anything."

I was sure I looked worried. Then he said in a calm voice, "Sergeant Kelly and I are not going to leave you here. If an attack comes, we will carry you back to our lines. If we are relieved, we will carry you back as we go."

I said, "I'm thirsty."

"I know, kid, but with a gut wound, nothing to eat or drink. Be still and try to get some rest. One of us will check you every hour or so. We won't leave you."

As Lieutenant Brown crawled away, I could make out most of what he was saying to himself: "Why did the round fall short? Who's so stupid he set the elevation short or figured the elevation wrong? What a pity, to be hit by friendly fire. . ."

Chapter Twelve

Lieutenant Brown was gone. His mumbling grew softer and softer until finally, I could hear nothing. I shut my eyes and said a prayer.

As a child, I had not gone to church. We didn't have a car, although, sometimes people would come by the house and offer to take us. Still, we didn't have any good clothes. I knew my mother would have felt out of place being in church with all the dressed-up people.

She bought me new pants and shirts and shoes each fall before school started. Most of my other clothes were given to me by Mrs. Boyd whose sons were two and three years older than me. Actually, she didn't give them to me; she brought them to my mother. Usually these were clothes that were outgrown. A lot of the clothes were nearly worn out, but sometimes the jackets and coats and boots were good.

Anyway, when I started my prayer, I didn't know what to say. I remembered the reading of the Bible and saying a prayer in school each morning. Someone in the class read a few verses from the Bible, then the class would recite the Lord's Prayer.

And we had a Bible at home. My mother said the church had given it to her and my father when they were married.

Mother told me that she didn't read it very often. My mother didn't read much at all. We didn't get the newspaper every day like a lot of people did, but sometimes neighbors would bring magazines. These were usually old Life and Look magazines. Sometimes they brought catalogues from Sears-Roebuck and Montgomery-Ward. I can remember her sitting by the lamp looking at the catalogues and the magazines. She used to do this while I was trying to do my school homework. When I went upstairs to bed, she was still looking at the catalogues. I always wished I could buy her all of the things she wanted to order from those catalogues.

When I was young and food was scarce, I didn't understand why my mother didn't have a job. Other women worked. Jay's mother worked in the post office. Joey's mother worked at the school in the cafeteria line. She collected lunch money every day. Mrs. Brent drove a school bus. Some of these women had husbands and children; some had no husbands, like my mother. I remember the time I asked my mother why she didn't have a job like other women. I told her, "It would really be nice to have a lot of food in the house."

But when I looked up at her, I saw tears running down her face. She used one hand, then the other to wiped away those tears, but they kept coming. It took a long time before she said anything, and I was sorry I had asked. Then she held out her arms, and I went to her and got in her lap. She held me real tight.

"When I was a little girl, I couldn't learn. I went to Wicomico School only for part of four years. You know where I mean, Son?"

I nodded.

"The teacher had told her mother that I would be better off staying home and helping her with the work at home."

My mother shivered a little bit. Then she told me that she was always sickly and caught cold. Her brothers told her she was dumb, and they made fun of everything she did.

"My father always told me I was not dumb. He told me if I kept trying to do things right, I would be able to do them. Then one day I met your father. He said he didn't care how I did things."

"I tried, oh, Lord, how I tried." She looked at me as if I didn't believe her. "We got by, but I was always sickly and I still can't do any heavy work."

I didn't know what to say. I was sorry I had said anything to my mother about working. I didn't want to make her cry. And it seemed like once she started talking she couldn't stop. She kept talking about how she tried lots of jobs, like the time she tried to stay with Mrs. Hill. Mrs. Hill had come home from the hospital after having an operation and her husband had asked if Mother would come and stay with her while she was recovering. He had told her she would have to do the cleaning, washing, ironing, cooking, and wait on Mrs. Hill. Mrs. Hill wasn't supposed to get out of bed for a week, and then she could only sit up in a chair. Mr. Hill told her he would be working on the water every day the weather was good, catching oysters. He would leave early and not get back until after dark. He told Mother she would have to feed and water the chickens, bring in the eggs, and feed and water the hogs. Mother told Mr. Hill she would like to have the job, and they agreed on a price. Mr. Hill said he would come for her when Mrs. Hill came home from the hospital.

In the meantime, Mother talked to her sister-in-law about my brother and me staying with her. She said fine, and it was all arranged. A day or two later, Mr. Hill came back and told Mother he would come for her early the next day. Then he would go to pick up Mrs. Hill.

"When we got to the Hill house, I went inside, and I had never seen such a mess. Mrs. Hill had been sick for a long time before going to the hospital, and she had been in the hospital for two weeks. I had visited Mrs. Hill on several occasions, the last time only several days before she went to the hospital."

"I couldn't believe the mess. Mr. Hill was not a cook at all and he was less of a cleaner. His dirty clothes were all over the house. No dishes had been washed. He had used the same pots and pans on the stove. The ashes in the wood stove were almost to the top. There was no electricity nor running water."

Mr. Hill said, "I know the place is a mess, but before Mrs. Hill had gone to have her operation, she was not able to do much work."

Mother said, "That's the way some men are. They can't do a thing for themselves. I hope I raise my boys better than that."

I put my arms around her neck and hugged her and I could feel her arms around me. She continued talking about the mess at the Hill house. She said she got sick after two days and had to come home, so I guess Mr. Hill got somebody else to help them. Mother said she wasn't able to do the heavy work.

I don't remember anything about being at my Aunt Alice's, and neither my brother nor I had ever mentioned anything again about Mother not working.

I still wasn't sure what to say in my prayer, so I asked God in Heaven to look out for my mother and my brother and Sergeant Kelly and Lieutenant Brown. I didn't know what to say about myself, so I said nothing.

Just then, I looked up at the sky. I could see a star shining through the broken clouds, then more light. There was probably a full moon behind the clouds. I was so tired, and my hands ached as I held them against the bandage. I didn't feel cold anymore, only sleepy and lonely. I just kept thinking, how did I get here? Me, a driver, hit by friendly fire and bleeding?

Chapter Thirteen

I didn't think I had been asleep long. Everything seemed the same: the darkness, the cold, the ache in my hands and my arms. I tried to move my right hand and arm with my left hand, but it ached too much. I thought moving my fingers would help, so I tried. As I raised the fingers of my right hand with my left, I could feel how cold they were. My fingers were like ice! Even with the pain, I forced myself to move first my fingers, then my hand, and finally my arm. It hurt plenty, but soon the feeling came back.

I tried to move the rest of me a little, but as I moved, I felt something wet on my hand. I figured moving my arm must have started the bleeding again, so I put my right hand back over the compress and pressed hard. I wondered how long I could stay there without medical help. I opened my eyes and looked up at the sky. The clouds were thicker, but the moon poked through here and there. I thought it seemed warmer, less windy. Maybe it would clear off. . .

To take my mind off things, I imagined I was back home. I always heard that if you were dying, your life passes before you. I didn't know if I was dying or not, but I was sure thinking about one of the worst things that ever happened to me.

It was a beautiful warm spring day. The sun was hot, but not too hot, and the breeze was warm. The trees were budding and the spring flowers were in full bloom. Mother had been talking about planting her garden and Mr. Jennings was out plowing.

In the creeks the crabs were shedding. Although they were small, they were very tasty when they were fried golden brown. I didn't have anything I had to do, so I was sitting on the cabin of Mr. Howe's boat, talking to him about not much of anything.

I happened to look up the path toward Mr. Howe's house in time to see a boy, a young man really, approaching. I didn't recognize him at first, but as he got closer, I knew it was my old coon-hunting buddy, Jay. He was now in college, and I wasn't even going to school anymore.

Jay was three years older than me. He hurried along the dock and climbed onto the boat and took a seat next to me. After exchanging greetings with Mr. Howe and me, he asked what the news was with us. I said, "Not much," fast as I could.

Mr. Howe blurted out, "What do you mean, B.B.?" That's what my friends always called me. Mr. Howe was quick to ask my friend if his father had told him about my problem with the law. What he actually said was, "Heard about B.B.'s trouble, didn't you?"

Jay said, "Yeah. I heard a little."

I knew his father, Jim Hopkins, had helped pay the lawyer, but I didn't know if anybody else besides him and Mr. Howe had paid the fee. I had no idea how much it was. I asked, but nobody answered me. They said it was no concern of mine. I didn't know what that meant. Mr. Howe told me not to bring it up again, but I was determined that one day I would pay it back, whatever the cost.

While I was thinking about the cost of the trial and paying off my debt to Mr. Howe and whoever else paid my expenses, Mr. Howe stopped working on his engine. He said,

"I am going to tell you what they tried to do to B.B. and if it hadn't been for your father and me, they may have pulled it off and B.B. would be in jail or the state pen."

Before he started to talk, he took out his bag of tobacco and a piece of cigarette paper to roll a homemade cigarette. He held the paper with the forefinger and thumb of his left hand and smoothed the paper with his right thumb and forefinger, then he poured tobacco from the bag. He tightened the drawstring with his right hand and held one side of the string with his front teeth. He smoothed the tobacco in the paper so there was an even amount. Then he folded the paper over several times to make it tight, even as tobacco fell out each end. He licked the paper to make it stick together. Then, sticking one end of the cigarette in his mouth, he took a kitchen match from his shirt pocket and scratched it on the engine box.

He took a long drag on the homemade cigarette, sat on the side of the engine box and began to tell the tale of my trouble with the law. Then he looked at me funny and said, "You tell him, B.B."

I began. Mother and I had gotten behind on the rent and couldn't pay, so we had moved in with a cousin of hers. This had happened before, but usually Mother would sell a piece of furniture. The owner of the house never asked us to leave, but we didn't want to owe money that we couldn't ever pay back.

Some of the conditions of moving in with our cousin was that I was to cut wood and keep the yard cut. We had only been at our cousin's house a few days when someone broke into the house down the road about a mile. No one was home at the time and we never really heard what was taken, but the next day the sheriff came around asking questions. He wanted to find out what we knew about the break-in. He said someone had seen a young boy come out of the house on the day of the robbery. I don't think he was even sure what day the house was robbed, since we had heard from other neighbors that the owner had been gone for a week. The robbery had taken place sometime while they were gone, but no one knew when for sure.

The sheriff came back on two more days and kept asking me what I was doing on certain days. I tried to tell him as best I could, but one day wasn't much different from the other. Mornings I'd cut wood and fill the wood box, then after lunch I'd pick up sticks and weed the garden. On the fourth visit, after asking a lot of questions, he told me and my mother that he thought I was the one who had broken into the house and he wanted to know what I had done with the things I had taken.

My mother started to cry, and I couldn't believe what I was hearing. I had never taken anything from anybody in my life. I thought of the times we were hungry, and I hadn't stolen from the Mr. Jackson's store. Now I was being accused of robbing a house I had never even been to. The sheriff kept saying I should come clean and tell him what I had done with the stuff I had stolen, and I kept telling him I had never been in that house.

He finally said he was taking me to jail. He said that would give me time to think it over. He reached into his pocket and took out a pair of handcuffs. He put them on me, held my arm tight, and marched me to his car.

As we approached the jail, I kept thinking about my mother. What would happen to her? She had no close family, and my big brother was in the army. She couldn't stay anywhere by herself and I didn't know if her cousin would let her stay there if I wasn't able to do the work as I had promised.

Who would bring in the wood for the cook stove and the other stoves to keep warm? Who would walk to the store when they needed food? Who would buy coal oil for the lamps, which were our only lights.

My only earnings this time of year were from an occasional job cleaning up yards. I got paid ten cents per hour, which wasn't too bad. A grown man worked ten or twelve hours per day at a saw mill for one dollar a day. I knew they would miss having this money, but then, I wouldn't have to eat. They would feed me as long as I was in jail.

I was still thinking about my mother as we approached the jail. I had seen the building before, but hadn't paid much attention to it. Now I did. The sheriff stopped in front of this brick building, which had two stories, bars on all the windows, and a metal door. It looked dreadful. The sheriff asked me again when I was going to show him the things I had stolen from the house. I kept telling him I hadn't broken into the house, I had never been to the house in my life.

The sheriff got out of the car, opened the rear door of the car, and took me by the arm. He said, "get out." The sheriff was a big man! I hardly came up to his shoulder. It had crossed my mind on the way to the jail to hit him in the head. There was no partition between the seats. If I had, maybe he would have run into the ditch, and I could have gotten away. But right then I was glad I had not done that. The sheriff got out a set of keys attached to a large key ring and opened the metal door. He didn't say a word as he held me by the arm. His coat was open, and I could see a gun—a pistol in a holster. I didn't attempt to run, but I was thinking about it.

Inside the jail, my eyes adjusted to the light, and all I could see were bars from the floor to the ceiling. The cells were made of barred partitions with doors of iron bars. There was a large lock on each door. Right then, I didn't notice how many cells there were, but now I recall there were six. There was no partition between any of the cells except the bars. I did see two people in the cells that day, but they didn't say anything.

The sheriff took another of his keys, opened a door, took me by the arm, and removed my handcuffs. Then he pushed me into a cell. As he closed the door, it banged. He just smiled and said, "Boy, you had better come clean."

I looked around the cell. There was a bunk hung from the wall by a chain at the foot and a chain at the head. The bunk was attached to the bars along one side. I found out later you could raise the bed up and clean under it. When you let it down, the chain made it level. There was a straw mattress on the bed. No sheets, but they did give you a blanket and a pillow. There were two buckets on the floor in the corner, both empty. I found out later that one was to wash in and the other was for a toilet. There was a small opening, big as two bricks laid sideways, in the door. Later I learned this was how you were fed. Someone would bring you a tray of food and hand it in to you through this space.

I sat on the bed for a while. I imagined it was about 4:00 in the afternoon since I had no watch and the jail had no clock I could see. I sat there on the bunk with my hands on my face, and my elbows on my knees. Then I started to cry.

A friendly voice said, "Things will be okay, son."

I raised my head up a little and saw an old black man standing in the cell next to me. I hadn't noticed, but the sheriff had gone. I didn't hear him open and close the big metal door. He said, "I can't help you get out, but maybe, just maybe, we can talk and that will help." He asked me my name, which I told him. Then he asked my father's name. I told him he was dead, had been for years. He asked me my mother's name. I told him. He seemed shocked. He said, "You are the folks that moved into the old Hanson place." I told him yes. He said, "Boy, what are you doing here?"

I told him about someone breaking into a house down the road and the sheriff thinking I had done it, which I hadn't.

He replied, "I know about that place and the break-in." I asked him his name. "My name is Bob Jones," he said, and he sounded real proud, "I make the best liquor around." When he said this I could see his chest rise and he showed an upper front gold tooth as he smiled. "A lot of people in the courthouse tells me I have the best liquor around."

This seemed surprising to a fifteen-year-old boy. I asked him why he was in jail. "Don't you know, son? There is an election coming and they have to have convictions so the people will think they're doing a good job."

He asked me if I had a lawyer.

I told him, "No."

He said, "Son, you need a lawyer. I've got one, and he will get me off with a fine. But, son, you need a lawyer."

I asked him how I'd get one.

He said, "Son, you got to have money."

I told him I didn't have any.

He said, "Without money and a lawyer, you're in trouble, son."

I don't know how long we talked or what else we talked about, but time passed quickly. It was beginning to get dark, and I was getting really hungry. I hadn't had any lunch. I told Bob Jones that I was really hungry.

He said, "It won't be long before food comes and it will be good."

Just then I heard a voice behind me. I had barely noticed the other person in the jail. The cell next to me on the left was empty, but this voice was from farther down the line. I guess this man had been lying on his bed, because I hadn't seen him. His voice was deep and scratchy, and not very friendly. At first I didn't want to listen to him, but I couldn't help hearing what he was saying.

"They ain't gonna give you no food until you confess, boy, and you might as well do it now."

Bob Jones cut into his conversation and said, "Don't tell the boy that; you know it isn't true."

Just then we heard the key in the big metal door. The key turned, the door opened and a man entered. I could smell food. A man whom I had never seen before had a basket covered by a big napkin. He set the basket on a table near the big metal door, removed the napkin, took out two trays, and began putting food from bowls on to the trays. He seemed like a friendly sort, and he and Bob Jones started to talk. He told Bob his portion would be short tonight, and the kid wouldn't get anything. Bob pleaded with him, telling him to please feed the boy, that he hadn't had lunch and not much breakfast. The man said he was sorry, but he had his orders.

I knew what was happening. They weren't going to give Bob a regular meal. They thought he might give some of it to me. The sheriff had said I wasn't to get anything. The man stayed until Bob and the other man had finished. After they ate, he took their trays, put them in the basket, turned toward me as he opened the door, and said, "So long, kid. Nothin' personal."

I sat down on the bed as he slammed the door shut. The man in the farthest cell hollered, "See, kid, I done told you so. No food until you confess."

Bob Jones walked over to the bars separating our cells and held out his big black hand which contained a biscuit. I ate it right down. Boy, was it good. I could have eaten a dozen more. I'll always remember the smile on his face. Neither Bob Jones nor I said anything, but I could see he knew how I felt.

It was almost dark, and there were no lights in the jail. I turned around and looked at the white man in the cell farther down the line. Evidently, he was looking at me, too. He knew the black man had given me something to eat, but I don't think he knew what. With an air of confidence, I asked him what he was in jail for. He snapped, "None of your business, kid, but you and I are going to be in the same pen—me for murder and you for stealing."

I turned around, bent down, took off my shoes, and lay on the bed. It was about dark. The only light was a street light outside the jail that showed through the windows. I shivered, but not because I was cold. It was because I was a fifteen-year-old kid in jail with a murderer and a bootlegger, held for a crime I hadn't committed.

Chapter Fourteen

The last thing I thought about as I dozed off was how hungry I was, and when I awoke, the sun's rays were shining in the eastern windows of the jail. My stomach was still empty, and it felt like it was digesting itself.

As I sat on the side of the bed putting on my shoes, Bob Jones said, "Good morning."

I said the same back to him. Then I heard from the other end of the jail, "What's good about it?"

Just then, the same man who had brought supper came with breakfast. He carried the food in the same basket covered with a checkered red and white napkin. I watched as he took containers of food out of the basket and put them on the table. This time he took out three trays. My stomach ached. I was so hungry. Eagerly I watched him separate the three trays and divide the food from the containers onto them. I couldn't wait to eat. The bacon smelled so good; the scrambled eggs looked like manna from heaven; and steam rose from the biscuits as he unwrapped them from another cloth.

The big metal outside door flung open and the sheriff waddled in. He didn't smile or greet the deputy. Instead he said harshly, "Have you fed the kid yet?"

The deputy half turned around smiling. "No, not yet, but it's all here and ready."

The sheriff said, "I told you not to feed him until he confesses."

The smile on the deputy's face faded quickly and he said, "You have got to feed the boy. He's hungry. You know his mother doesn't have much to feed him and my wife fixed him an especially good breakfast."

The sheriff told the deputy to remember who was the boss. He said I was not going to get fed until I confessed. Then he pointed his finger toward my face and bellowed, "Kid, I've got you now! If you confess to stealing, that plate of food is yours!"

My eyes kept going from his finger to the tray of food. Next to me, Bob Jones was eating. I heard him crunching the bacon, and I could smell it like it was mine. The hunger pains were worse than ever, as I faced the sheriff's finger stabbing at me in the air. It was a short, stubby, dirty finger.

I looked the sheriff in the eye and said softly, "Okay, I'll confess if I can eat." The sheriff smiled, "You don't eat until you sign the confession." Then he took his large key ring from his belt and opened my cell door. He told me to hold out my arms, and he reached into his pocket and took out handcuffs and locked them around my wrists. "We've got to catch the Commonwealth Attorney and have him write up the confession for you to sign before he goes to court today."

He marched me from the jail to another office in another building, almost pulling me along. I was weak from hunger, but he seemed friendlier than before. The office was small: only one story and in need of paint inside and out. There was a lady sitting at a small black desk between two filing cabinets. The drawers were open and papers were jammed into them. The sheriff greeted her in a real friendly manner and she smiled back. It was easy to see they were old friends.

With a smile of satisfaction on his face, the sheriff said,

"This young man wants to confess to the break-in down the road." She seemed surprised, but she said, "That is great news, Sheriff. Glad you solved that, and it won't hurt your chances of reelection either."

From a room behind the desk, I heard a booming voice say, "Congratulations, Sheriff! I thought that was going to be a hard case to solve." A larger smile appeared on the sheriff's face. "Ellen will type it up, and the young man can sign it. I'll try to get the judge to act on it today. You know this is court day."

The sheriff answered, "Of course, I do. I have to appear in six cases."

The lady typed some things, asking the sheriff for information from time to time. The man in the back room kept talking to the sheriff. I couldn't see him, but the sheriff could. Before long, the lady had typed the half page. She took it out of the typewriter and handed it to the sheriff. He read it over and said it was okay. He called to the man in the back room and asked him if he was ready to witness. I didn't know what that meant, but the man said he was on his way.

A small man dressed in a dark suit appeared at the door of the office. "All right, have him sign it." He put the paper in front of me, and the lady handed me a pen. The man in the dark suit asked the sheriff if I could read.

The sheriff replied, "It doesn't make any difference if he can read. He has already confessed."

The small man said, "We just have to keep it legal, Fred." I read it hurriedly but my mind was on food. The lady showed me where to sign and I signed. It was difficult to write with handcuffs on.

"By the way, does this young man have counsel?"

"No," relied the sheriff. "But that shouldn't be any problem. It's an open and shut case."

The sheriff took me by the arm and led me out of the office and back to the jail. As we walked along, he was almost friendly. "You did the right thing." I looked him right in the eye and said again I had not broken into the house. He looked surprised. He said, "You had to. You were the only person who could have done it."

"But I didn't," I insisted. I don't know how many times I had told him that I had never ever been to that house, but this was the first time I saw doubt in his eyes.

His uncertainty didn't last long. He said now I could have all I wanted to eat. As soon as the sheriff opened the big metal door, I could smell the bacon. He reached into his pocket and took out a key and removed the handcuffs. He pointed his dirty, stubby finger toward the opened cell door and told the deputy to feed me.

The food was cold, but did it taste good! The deputy told me not to eat too fast. I tried to eat as slowly as I could, but it was hard to not gobble. I washed it down with the cold coffee.

When I looked up, the sheriff was gone. The deputy was packing up the trays and the containers he had brought the food in. He looked at me and asked if I was finished. I answered, "Yes, sir."

"Well, hand me the tray," he said. I had been sitting on the side of the bed eating. Quickly I got up, handing him the tray through the slot in the door and thanked him. He smiled, put my tray in the basket, and left.

I was still worried, but I felt better now that I wasn't so hungry, so I lay down on the bed. When I looked up, I saw Bob Jones looking down at me. He wasn't smiling this time.

"Did they make you sign?"

I told him I had signed.

"How much time will you get?"

I didn't know what he was talking about.

He said, "I am talking about you being in jail for a year or in the penitentiary for several years."

"You think that's going to happen to me?" I asked.

"Yes, you admitted you robbed that house," he said.

"But I didn't!"

"That's not what the paper you signed says."

"What am I going to do?" Tears ran down my cheeks.

Bob put out his long arm and touched my shoulder. "I am sorry, son. I guess I should have told you what they were going to do to you."

"Tell me what will happen now."

"Well," Bob took his hand from my shoulder and sat on his bed. "First they will take you to the courtroom. They will ask you lots of questions. There will be a jury, but this is not the jury that will send you to the pen. This jury is called a grand jury. I don't know what makes it 'grand,' but that is what they call it. Then you will come back to jail if they think you could have done it and wait for the trial unless you can get bail. If you can get bail, you can go home until the trial."

"What is bail?" I asked.

"That's when somebody puts up money for you, saying that you will be here for the trial. The judge will tell you what the bail is. Do you have any money?"

"No. Neither does my mother."

"What about anybody else?"

"No. There is nobody else."

"Well, I guess you will have to stay in jail. Anyway, the time you spend in jail now should count against your total time." Bob looked at me like a father would look at his son and said, "Let me tell you what happened to me. I have been through this six times, so I guess this time won't be any different."

"First time I got caught selling homemade applejack. We had a nice crop of apples that year and it made good juice. I don't add nothin' to the juice but sugar and yeast and let nature take its course. Anyway, it's a lot better than working at the sawmill for a dollar a day and what they feed you. I make it just like my father did, and he taught me good. They say his juice was the best."

"Anyway, I go before this jury, the grand one, and they

ask a lot of questions and they have other people who knew about what I did come and talk. Then the jury goes into a room and votes on whether they think I could have done what they said I did. If they think you could have done it, then the judge will set a day for the trial before the real jury.

"But, son, my lawyer is always there to help me not get mixed up and say something I shouldn't. Of course, he's on my side. He's one of my best customers, but I never charge him, and I don't have to pay him either. He will take care of the bail, too, if I want to get out. He and his partner, who died several years ago, used to help all of us boys during prohibition. Now it's all right for the state store to sell whiskey, but us boys, well, we aren't supposed to make the money. It's still better than working at the sawmill though. Mr. Nance, my lawyer, could get me out on bail, but I am probably going to get thirty days in jail like last time, so this is a good time to go on and serve part of my time. I don't know what they mean when they say I owe the state this time in jail. Half of the people in that courthouse buy my juice. They drink it and they say it's good. No, sir, I don't understand that at all.

"When you have the trial and the jury votes on you, the judge will tell you how much time you have to give the state. Of course, in your case, you have already said you broke in, so I don't know how that works. Mr. Nance always tells me to tell them I am not guilty. Sometimes he can talk to the jury and they're not sure that I am guilty. I always am guilty, but sometimes saying I'm not helps. It depends on the jury— whether they believe you or not. I never try to lie too much because they usually know you are lying."

"Son, I wish I could help you, but I can't. When you go to your trial, just tell the truth. That is all I can say, and the Lord be with you."

Bob's eyes, had tears in them. He wanted to help me, but I guess he knew he couldn't.

I had forgotten all about the other guy in the jail, when

he boomed out, "Kid, I told you we would be in the pen together. Maybe we could be cell mates." Then he laughed real loud.

We heard a key turning in the big metal door, and the deputy came in with a bundle of wrinkled clothes in his arms. He went over to Bob's cell and began to shove the clothes through the space where the food trays were passed. Smiling, he said, "Your wife walked up home last night and brought your suit of clothes. You know you go to trial this morning."

Bob was smiling as he unrolled his suit. "Wish I had a hook to hang this on. Got to look my best." The deputy smiled at Bob and asked him how many times this made for him to go to court.

"Can't rightly say, but I think it's six." Bob's smile faded, his voice turned serious and he said to the deputy. "I was trying to tell this fella what would happen to him. Can't you tell him? I'm not sure."

The deputy put his hand behind his head and sighed, "Well, first of all he will go before the grand jury. As he has confessed, they will return a true bill. Then a trial date will be set and there will probably be a jury. Without a lawyer to help and since he has confessed, I just don't know."

The deputy turned toward me. He wasn't smiling any more. He just shook his head and walked toward the door. He called over his shoulder, "I will be back with dinner shortly."

Bob changed into his suit. He was ready for his trial, and confident that he would be out of jail and at home that afternoon. I kind of wished he was going to stay in jail with me. He had been like a father to me, and I liked that.

Chapter Fifteen

While I talked about my brush with the law, Mr. Howe rolled one cigarette after another and smoked them down until they were almost burning his lips. The fingers on his right hand were yellow from tobacco, and I was thinking maybe the sheriff's fingers had been tobacco stained, not dirty.

"Come on, B.B. Tell the rest," said Mr. Howe.

"Well," I said, "Bob Jones left with the deputy to go to the court house." He had told me before he left that he would be back for dinner. Then looking back at me, he said, "If you leave before I get back, I'll try to see you later."

It wasn't long before Bob returned and said that his case was over and he was going home. His lawyer had him plead guilty, and he got fifteen days in jail, but since he had already been in jail for two weeks they told he could go home after dinner. He said he would go by and tell my mother I was all right. I asked him to tell her I would be home soon. He stopped smiling, but he agreed to tell her.

When dinner came, it was good. Bob said they always had good food on court days and plenty of it. He told a tale of a man gaining twenty pounds during his forty-five days in jail. The man was used to doing hard work, and in jail he didn't do anything. He had said the hardest thing he ever did in jail was put the food in his mouth and chew it.

After dinner, when the deputy came to get the dishes, Bob asked if he could go. The deputy smiled and said, "Certainly. The door isn't locked but the sheriff said to be sure you got dinner before you went home."

"I know what that means," Bob whispered. Before he left, he explained, "That will cost me a quart of my liquor, but I guess it's a fair trade. My wife doesn't know I am coming home today, and I have a four-mile walk unless I can get a ride." Then Bob said good-bye and was gone.

The deputy was at the table behind the big metal door filling out some forms. I noticed the other prisoner had gone somewhere, too. I hadn't seen him leave, so I asked the deputy where he was. He said he had gone to the court house to appear before the grand jury. He said I had been asleep when he left. I couldn't remember going to sleep, but I had been lying down on the bunk most of the morning. And what difference would it make anyway? I didn't ever want to talk to this man. Still, with Bob gone, I didn't have anyone to talk to except the deputy.

All of a sudden, the big metal door handle turned and the sheriff held the door open for a small man wearing two-toned shoes and a white suit. He carried a fancy straw hat in his hand. The sheriff was telling him I had confessed to the break-in and that it wouldn't do any good to talk to me, but the deputy jumped to his feet, picked up his papers, and held them to his chest.

I had no idea who this man was, until the deputy called him Mr. Nance.

He had a broad smile, and I could see several gold teeth in the back of his mouth. The sheriff told him again I had confessed already, but this man, still smiling, said, "Gentlemen, I want to have a word in private with my client if you will be so good."

The sheriff kept repeating, "But he confessed, and he

don't have no money." But the man just smiled and said, "Yes. That is very true, but his friends have money, and they don't believe he robbed the house. I am to represent him."

"But what about the confession?" the sheriff asked.

"Well, gentlemen, the court will decide the case, not you or I. Please let me talk alone to this nice young man. He will go before the grand jury this afternoon, and I have to prepare my case."

"But . . . the confession!" exclaimed the sheriff.

The smile disappeared from Mr. Nance's lips. "Oh, yes. I read his confession this morning, but I didn't believe it, nor do his friends who are paying my bill. The court will decide this case, Sheriff Hughes. Now, gentlemen, please let me talk alone to my client."

The sheriff said, "Okay. Where do you want to talk?"

"Right here is fine as long as there is no one else here."

The sheriff said, "Fine. I have to go to court at 2:00 P.M." He looked at his watch. "It's almost that now. That's the murder case. I won't be back for at least an hour."

"That should be plenty of time to get to know this young man."

The sheriff told Mr. Nance that the big metal door was unlocked. He said he could leave when he wanted, but that his client's cell was locked. Then they walked out.

"That's okay," Mr. Nance said. "All we want to do is talk." Then he smiled again and asked me to shake his hand. He stuck it through the space where food was passed. He said his name was Mr. Nance and that my friends had retained him to represent me. After our handshake, he stepped back, moved the deputy's table and a chair next to the cell, took a pen from his shirt pocket, held it between his teeth to undo the top, and removed several sheets of paper from his inside coat pocket. As he unfolded them, I could see some writing on them, but I couldn't read any of the words.

His first words to me were, "Boy, you are in one helluva mess, but I will do everything I can to help you. Now, there is one thing I must know, and I want the truth. No matter what answer you give me, I will still help you, but I have to know the truth. Did you break into that house?"

I looked him in the eye and said, "No, sir, I did not break into that house."

"Well, why did you confess to it?"

I said, "You mean that paper I signed?"

"Yes!" Mr. Nance hit his fist on the table.

"Don't you know? They wouldn't feed me until I signed that paper? I was so hungry."

Mr. Nance jumped to his feet and said, "You mean the sheriff wouldn't feed you until you confessed?" Then he muttered under his breath, "I knew there would be a close election this year, but the sheriff had no business doing that!"

When he sat down again, he asked me to tell him in detail as well as I could remember what was said and who said it. He wrote down most everything I said.

Then he said, "We will go to court this afternoon before the grand jury. All I want you to do is tell the truth, and I will do the very best I can for you. Now, I want you to know what to expect, but I can't tell you what questions I am going to ask. The Commonwealth Attorney will ask you questions also. Don't add anything to your answers. Just say, 'Yes, sir,' or 'No, sir.' What will probably happen is that the grand jury will find there is probable cause for a trial. That's when we will bring out about your not being fed until you confessed. They will probably ask you why you signed a confession. Tell them that you didn't know what it meant. They will ask you if you read what you signed. Tell them that you read it, but didn't know what it meant."

He then asked me how far I got in school. I told him the sixth grade. I noticed he wrote that down in his notes. He also told me that the trial would be in a month if all went as he thought it would.

Then came the big surprise. He put on his straw hat, folded his papers, and put them in an inside coat pocket.

With one hand on the big metal door, he turned toward me smiling and said, "I think the judge will let you go home this afternoon."

By this time, his back was toward me, so I hollered after him to ask what he meant. Again he turned toward me with a grin and said, "I hope you can go home this afternoon. I am going to ask the judge to grant bail. Your friends have put up the money, and I think the judge will agree."

Well, the sheriff came back to the jail about 2:30 P.M. and told me I was to go to court with him immediately to appear before the grand jury. The sheriff put handcuffs on me and told me to walk along with him. As we got to the court house steps, he asked me again, real quietly, if I had broken into that house.

I said, "No, sir, I did not break into that house."

Then I heard him mumble, "Maybe I did make a mistake."

As we climbed the stairs to the second floor of the court house, I felt like my stomach was about to drop, and the sweat started running down my face. My legs didn't want to go where I put them, and my heart was beating so hard against my chest that it hurt.

The sheriff looked at me with some concern and said, "It won't be so bad, son."

At the top of the stairs, the deputy was standing outside the double doors into the court room. He told the sheriff that the other case was over. So the sheriff and deputy pushed open one of the doors and led me in. This was my first time ever in a court room.

In the back of the room were about five benches. There were people on some of these but nobody I knew or had ever seen before. There was also a step up with a railing between the benches and two large tables with shiny tops. Stacks of paper and books were lying on the tables, and it didn't look to me like they were in any particular order. The deputy told me to sit at a certain table, and the sheriff removed the handcuffs.

The man from the office where I signed the confession came in. He and the sheriff began talking quietly. I couldn't tell what they said, but the sheriff had a worried expression. Then the man sat at the other table.

I looked around the room. There was a high thing, like a desk. The top of it was as high or higher than my head. Next to that was a chair with a step up to it, and on the other side was a lower desk not anything like as big as what was in the middle. Then on the far right was a section with a railing around it, and in it were twelve big chairs.

The U.S. flag was there, too. We always said the pledge of allegiance to it in school each morning. And I saw the Virginia flag was there, too, and on the walls, back and side, were all these pictures of men dressed up in old clothes. There was even one picture of a woman.

Just then Mr. Nance came in and smiled. I felt better just seeing him. He came over and sat in a chair next to me. He asked me if I had ever been to court before. I told him I hadn't. He quickly told me where the judge would sit, where the clerk of the court would sit, where the jury would sit, and where the witness would sit to answer questions. Then he told me what would happen. The judge would ask me if I pleaded guilty or not guilty. "Say not guilty," he said, and "Always add sir."

A few minutes later, the jury took their seats. Then the judge came in wearing a black robe. Then another man got up and said something. He talked so fast I couldn't understand him except for his first words which were, "Hear ye, hear ye." Then the same man read something about the state versus me. The judge asked the man at the other table a question, and he showed the paper I had signed to the judge.

When Mr. Nance got his turn he said the confession should be set aside. He told them I didn't know what I had signed, nor did I understand the meaning of what I had signed. The man at the other table kept getting up and repeating that I had confessed to the crime. Mr. Nance told the judge it was true I had signed the confession, but he said again that I did not understand what I had signed. After all this, the judge asked me how I pleaded.

I looked up at Mr. Nance. I didn't know what that meant. Mr. Nance told the judge that I didn't understand the question. Then the judge said, "Did you rob that house, or not?"

I said, "No, sir, I did not."

The judge said, "A person has a right to change his plea, but I think the grand jury has to take into account the signed confession."

Mr. Nance stood up and said in a clear voice, "Your honor, we will welcome the chance to talk about the confession in a court of law."

The judge asked the grand jury if they had any questions. None of them did. Then they got up and went into a back room. The judge also went into a back room, but Mr. Nance kept his seat next to me.

"They won't be long," he said. "I expect them to bring in what is called a true bill. There isn't anything else they can do now with the confession you signed."

The jury wasn't out ten minutes. When everybody was back in the court room, that was exactly what happened. The judge set a date for my trial, and Mr. Nance asked that bail be set for me. I remember him saying that the bail should be low, that I was no danger to the state, that I had never been out of the county. The judge set bail at $100.

Mr. Nance told me I was free to go home, but he said I had to be there for the trial. He said I would have to answer questions on the witness stand, and that all I had to do was to tell the truth. The last thing he said was, "Be sure to wear a suit and tie when you come to the trial."

Mr. Howe said to Jay, "Doesn't that beat all? They really tried to get B.B., didn't they?" and he rolled another cigarette. I thought about all the times Mr. Howe had talked about the trial, but he always enjoyed it. I knew he had helped pay for Mr. Nance, but he would never tell me how much.

As I started down the stairs of the court house, I heard a deep, gruff voice call my name. "Wait up," someone said. It was the sheriff. He told me to be sure that I was there the day of my trial. Again he asked me if I had robbed that house. I told him no and also that I had never been to that house.

"Well, I don't know how your lawyer is going to prove it."

I didn't answer.

"What is your plan?"

I looked the sheriff square in the face and said, "Mr. Nance told me to just tell the truth."

The sheriff made no comment.

Chapter Sixteen

I was half asleep, sort of dozing, when Sergeant Kelly tugged at my shoulder. He said, "I could hear you talking, but I couldn't understand what you were saying. It was something about a trial?"

"I guess I was dreaming."

"Well, anyway, how are you doing?"

"I'm not cold, but I feel like I'm sweating. I am so thirsty."

"Let me give you enough water to wet your lips, but don't swallow."

"I can't get to my canteen."

"I can reach mine." With that, he poured some water in his cup and held it to my lips. It was only a few drops, but it tasted good. I tried to raise my arm to hold the cup with my hand, but it was numb and it tingled as I tried to raise it.

"I'll hold it," Sergeant Kelly said. "Keep your hand on the compress. And by the way, you can call me Kelly. You don't have to say Sergeant Kelly. All my friends call me Kelly."

"Where is the lieutenant?" I asked.

"He just relieved me. I came to the rear to check on you and to get a little rest. Do you feel like talking?"

"I guess I do."

"Do you want to tell me about your dream?"

"I can talk about the trial. It wasn't a dream. It really happened to me." Kelly was a kind person, and I felt close to him even though we had only been on this observation post for three days, I think. I had been hit by the shell fragment the day before, I think, but it didn't matter. Each day, each night felt the same as the others.

I asked Kelly if I could wet my lips again. He gave me about five drops of water, and it felt good.

I told Kelly about being arrested and put in jail. I told him about not being fed until I confessed and about going before the grand jury.

"If you feel like it, tell me about your trial," he said.

"Let me tell you first about going home after going before the grand jury.

"Mr. Nance got me freed on bail," I began.

I told him that after I left the courthouse, I went back to the jail with the deputy to get what clothes I had, which weren't many. Mother had sent me a clean shirt and pants.

"As we walked along, he asked me how it felt to be free.

I told him, "Great."

"Remember, you are only free until your trial."

I looked at him and said, "But I didn't do it."

"I believe you. I just hope the jury will believe you." Then he smiled. "If you wait about half an hour, I'll take you home."

"Okay," I said.

As I opened the door to the jail he smiled and said, "Get your things. The cell door isn't locked. I'll be ready to go in about two minutes. I've just got to finish this paperwork."

I went into the cell to gather my clothes, then I got out of that cell. Being in jail those three days was the worst experience of my life. It was the first time I had ever been away from home. I don't mean to say that I hadn't ever been away from my mother. I had spent nights with my aunt when Mother went to work one time, and several times I had gone to help my cousin for a couple of days at a time. Mother and I had moved many times, so I really had no place to call home. Home was only a place where we lived. Home was being with my mother and my dog.

When the deputy was ready to go, he opened the big heavy iron door and told the man in the end cell that he would soon be back with his supper. In his harsh voice, the man said, "Okay and tell that kid that he ain't out of the woods yet. He's gonna be my roommate at the state pen!"

As the deputy closed the heavy door he said, "Don't you pay any attention to him. He's probably going to the electric chair, but Mr. Nance will do all he can for you. And by the way, don't tell anybody how Mr. Nance is going to handle your case."

"I already have, I guess. The sheriff asked me my plan. I told him Mr. Nance told me to just tell the truth."

"Well, that's fine. There's nothing the matter with what you told him."

Then the deputy drove me home. As he pulled onto the dirt lane leading to my cousin's house and approached the house, I saw my mother standing in the doorway. As soon as the deputy stopped the car, I opened the door and ran as hard as I could. My mother opened the screen door and held out her arms. Boy, was I glad to see her! With all the excitement, I didn't realize she was crying. I was, too, I guess. My dog, Lollipop, heard my voice and came running and barking, I leaned down to pet her, and she licked me in the face. Boy, she was glad to see me, but I am sure to this day that I was just as glad to see her.

As I stood up, my mother said that the deputy had been by and told her that I would probably be home that afternoon. I didn't know how he knew, but I was glad he thought about my mother. She also told me that the deputy had told her about Mr. Nance being my attorney. Thank goodness for Mr. Howe and whoever else put up the money.

I waved good-bye to the deputy just as my cousin called from the kitchen, "Supper's ready!"

She, too, had a big smile. Everybody was so glad I was home. I tried to explain that the trial would be in two weeks and that I might be found guilty and have to go to jail for a while, but Mother kept saying, "But I know you didn't break into that house. You were here all the time except when you went to the store, and that house is the other way from here. So you just couldn't. They'll see. My boy didn't do it."

Even with all the excitement of the day, I was lying in bed with my arm around my dog's neck, thinking about what might lay ahead for me. I had not told Mother about the confession. I had no idea what questions Mr. Nance was going to ask me, but I remembered what Bob Jones had told me about being on the witness stand and Mr. Nance not letting the other side get him mixed up. Like me, Mr. Nance had told him to just tell the truth.

I soon slept and it was morning before I knew it. At breakfast, my mother thought it would be a good idea for me to go to Mr. Howe's and see if I could help him. She said I could stay there with Mrs. Howe and help out. That way I would be out of the area where the robbery occurred. She said, "Maybe you could stay with the Howes until the trial, but don't go today. I want to have you with me for a couple of days."

Two days later I went to visit Mr. Howe. During those two days, I worked around the yard picking up tree branches that had fallen during the winter, raking up leaves and putting them where the garden would be. Also, I cut and stacked the remaining wood in the wood pile. This time of year my cousin didn't need much wood. What was used was mainly for cooking, but I had to get the bark and branches cleaned up so I could cut grass.

The Howes were sure glad to see me, and they asked

me to stay with them until the trial. It was a busy time for Mr. Howe, getting his crab pots made and rigged up with lines, weights, and corks. It was hard work, especially with his one leg. I did all I could to help him and Mrs. Howe, too. I brought in water and chopped wood for the cook stove. Mr. Howe really had a hard time trying to use that ax. He said, "Having only one leg really puts my balance off."

I was tired out from talking, so I asked Kelly if I could have a few more drops of water. He said yes, just to wet my lips. Then I asked him if he wanted to hear more.

"Yes, if you feel up to it, but don't get too tired. Rest if you want to."

"No," I told him. "I'm all right. I just can't feel my hands."

"Well, try not to move them. You've got to keep pressure on your wound to keep it from bleeding." We could still hear artillery shells exploding in the distance both to our front and to our rear.

I said, "Nothing much happened while I was at Mr. Howe's house waiting for the trial. Then on the big day, some of Mr. Howe's friends came and picked us up." Mr. Howe didn't have his own car, and when they came, I wondered if these men had helped to pay for Mr. Nance, too.

Two days before the trial, I had been down the river in the boat with Mr. Howe. We stopped at the dock where all the boats in the area bought gas. Up the hill from the dock was a large store where almost anything you wanted or needed from food to clothes to boat supplies, toys, and dishes were sold. You name it, they had it.

Mr. Howe told one of the clerks I wanted to buy a suit. I must have looked funny, I guess because Mr. Howe reassured me and told me it was all right. It had been taken care of. From that, I knew that Mr. Howe had either paid for my purchase or had arranged for credit. I tried to tell Mr. Howe that I had a suit at home.

"That's too small, I'm sure," he said, "and besides, you have to look your best."

After trying on the clothes, Mr. Howe picked what he thought would be suitable. He told the clerk to give me a new white shirt, too, and a tie and some new shoes, too. I didn't know what Mr. Nance had told Mr. Howe about how I should dress, but it was clear Mr. Nance had told me to dress up for the trial.

This was real nice, but even then I thought maybe it was too much. How was I ever going to pay for those clothes? I looked at Kelly. "The thing was, it was my first new suit. All my other clothes were given to me by mothers of older boys in the neighborhood. My mother bought me some new shirts and pants, but not often.

"On the day of the trial, I was all dressed up riding in the car with Mr. Howe, Jim and two other friends of Mr. Howe's." I looked at Kelly again. "You know it made me feel real grown up. But I felt small riding on the backseat sitting between those two big men."

We were at the court house about half an hour before the trial. Upstairs in the court room, Mr. Nance was looking over some papers spread out on the big shiny table in front of him. When he saw us come in, he got up with a broad grin on his face and walked over and shook hands with our group—including me. He asked particularly how I was. He said he had some questions about several of the potential jurors and asked one of the men in our group to look at the names. They went over to the shiny table with the scattered papers, and I heard the man named Jim tell Mr. Nance that he thought all but two of the people were all right. Mr. Nance smiled and said he would take care of them. I didn't know what that meant, but I found out later. He asked that they be excused from the jury.

The court came to order just like it had for the grand jury session except there was no jury in the room yet. People were called in one at a time, and the man at the other table,

Mr. Jewell, the judge called him, and Mr. Nance asked each one some questions. Some were told to take a seat in the jury box. Some were excused.

Once the jury was picked, the judge asked each lawyer to make an opening statement. Mr. Jewell went first. He said there was really no question about guilt because I had signed a confession admitting I had robbed that house. He made a big issue about the paper I had signed and kept holding it up so the jury could see it. He also said his only witness would be the sheriff.

Next, Mr. Nance made his opening statement. He said the confession meant nothing because the boy, who only had a sixth grade education, did not know what he was signing and had not been fed until he had signed the confession. Then the sheriff was called to the witness stand. Mr. Jewell asked him some questions. He talked about the confession and his investigation and said he was sure I had robbed that house, but he did say that he was unable to find what was missing from the house. Then Mr. Jewell told the judge that the state rested.

I asked Mr. Nance what that meant. He said the sheriff was the only witness against me. Mr. Nance hadn't asked the sheriff any questions. That seemed odd to me, but I thought Mr. Nance knew what he was doing.

The judge then told Mr. Nance to present his case. Mr. Nance leaned over to me and said, "Young man, just tell the truth."

They told me to take the oath. I didn't know what that meant.

The clerk had me raise my right hand and put my left hand on the Bible and promise to tell the truth.

I needed a break from talking, so I asked Kelly if I could wet my lips again. My mouth was so dry. It had been dry the day I was called to the witness stand, too. Kelly asked me if I was tired and wanted to rest, but I told him I would like to tell about the rest of the trial. He gave me a few drops of water again, and I moved my shoulders just a little. Changing my position—even a little—helped.

"Where was I, Kelly?"

"You were about to take the witness stand."

Mr. Nance asked me my name and address. I didn't know why, because he already knew it, but I guess he had a reason. He asked me if I was in school. I told him no. He asked me how far I had gotten in school.

I replied, "The sixth grade."

He also wanted to know why I had quit school, and I tried to explain to him that I was helping my mother, that she wasn't too well and couldn't work. He asked me how we supported ourselves. I told him about the allotment from my brother who was in the army. He asked me if my mother was in the court room. I told him no, she wasn't well enough. I didn't know why he asked me about my mother, because that didn't have anything to do with breaking into that house.

Mr. Nance went back to his table and looked through the scattered papers on the table until he picked out the paper he wanted. He showed it to the judge, and then he showed it to me. He asked me if I knew what the paper said. I read it over and saw at the bottom of the page where I had signed it. I told Mr. Nance that it was the paper I had signed in Mr. Jewell's office.

Mr. Nance was quick with his question.

"Why did you sign it?"

I blurted out, "They wouldn't feed me and told me they wouldn't until I signed a paper saying I had broken into that house."

Without hesitation, Mr. Nance asked, "Did you break into that house?"

I looked Mr. Nance right in the eye as I had the sheriff and said, "No, sir, I didn't break into that house. I have never stolen anything."

Then Mr. Nance had me tell about not being fed and how hungry I was. It was easy to tell this because I had had a big breakfast that morning. Mr. Nance asked me again if I broke into that house.

I said, "No, sir, I did not."

Then the Commonwealth Attorney started asking questions. He asked me if I signed that paper willingly. I told him that the sheriff wouldn't let the deputy feed me until I signed that paper.

He kept saying, "You admitted breaking into that house by signing that paper," and he waved it high in his hand.

Mr. Nance told the judge that that was not the question. He said, "We admit that this young man signed the confession, but I think it has been brought out how the sheriff got the signature on that paper."

Then Mr. Jewell said he didn't have any more questions. The judge asked for them to sum up the evidence or something like that. Mr. Jewell went first. He just talked about the confession.

Mr. Nance also talked on about the confession. He wasn't talking to the judge but to the jury. He went right up into their faces and kept pointing his finger and saying, "How would you like to have your brother or father or maybe yourself not fed until you signed a confession?"

He made a lot about none of the stuff from the house being found. In the end, he said, "The boy was accused and not fed until he signed a confession and therefore the state has no case. You must find him innocent."

Mr. Nance came back and sat in his chair near me at the shiny table. The judge talked to the jury and then they left the room. So did the judge. Mr. Howe and my other friends came around the table with me. Mr. Nance told them, "The jury won't take long. It's just a question of them believing this boy. I sure do." He patted me on my back, and I could see his gold teeth shining through his big smile.

Mr. Nance was right. The jury didn't stay out long. I heard someone say, "Tell the judge. The jury is back."

All were soon present and the room was quiet. The judge

asked the jury if they had reached a verdict. One man spoke for them and said that they had. The judge asked what the verdict was.

The man said, "Not guilty."

The judge said some words that I didn't understand and then hit his desk with a hammer. He said, "Court is adjourned."

Mr. Nance leaned over to me and said, "Son, you did it. We won and you are free!"

Mr. Howe and my friends came over and shook my hand and Mr. Nance's and thanked him, then they said, "Let's get out of here."

When we got downstairs and out on the porch, all the men lit cigarettes. Mr. Howe didn't roll his own this time but took a cigarette from someone else.

Mr. Jewell came down behind us. When the man named Jim saw him enter the porch, he went over to him and called him every name in the book and told him what a terrible person he was for trying to railroad "this boy." He kept pointing to me. Mr. Jewell said he had been wrong and was sorry. He went down the court house steps quickly with his head bowed low.

I looked to see if Kelly had been listening. When he smiled, I said, "You see, Kelly, this was my only brush with the law, and I didn't break into that house."

Chapter Seventeen

When I finished telling the story about my trial, I felt sad. Some people would have called it homesickness, but I knew I felt sad. I could feel the tears coming down my cheeks.

"How about a few drops of water?" Kelly asked.

"That would be fine," I answered.

I don't know how he poured a few drops into his canteen cup, but he did it, even in the dark. As he raised the cup to my lips, we heard artillery shells exploding nearby. The shells were from our guns. We could see the fire. It seemed to be almost continuous, and we wondered if our side was starting an attack?

Soon the enemy started shelling our lines, too. I lay as low in my foxhole as I could and I called for Kelly. When he didn't answer, I was sure he had gone to his foxhole. To each side, I saw the sky light up. I couldn't see behind, but from what I heard overhead, I was sure the enemy was shelling our area. Luckily, the shells weren't landing where we were.

I searched my mind for something real good to think about, and what came to me was I remembered Mr. Jackson's store. It was a two story building with a porch on the front. There were about five steps up to the porch—or was it six steps? No, it was five. The store had double doors, with two long windows on either side. The store was a gathering place for the people in the area after they visited the post office which was across the road.

I remembered that warm August afternoon that I was walking from the post office toward home and Mr. Jackson, the owner and operator of the store, called to me to please come there. I had no idea what he wanted, but he was always pleasant and helped my family in any way he could.

When I went to buy bacon—let's say it had ten cents a pound stuck on it—he would slice the slab of side meat— home-cured bacon—but he never took the time to weigh it. I always knew it was much more than a pound he gave me.

Or if I was buying two cans of something, I would get home and find three cans in the bag. One time I told him I only wanted two cans. He told me in all seriousness that he was having a sale and three cans were the same price as two.

It wasn't just me he helped either. He would let the children in the neighborhood get the eggs from his fowl coop and exchange them for candy or soft drinks. Some people would bring in eggs their hens had laid to exchange for credit. I remember Howard Beane, the local troublemaker, bringing in eggs that he found in the mangers where the horses were fed in the big barn behind his house. Mr. Jackson used to shake them to make sure they weren't rotten. Sometimes people would bring chickens, geese, and ducks to sell to him. He would give them credit for their fowl and later ship the fowl to Baltimore by truck.

I didn't know what he wanted this day, but I was always glad to go to the store. A lot of people hung around there. In the summertime, they sat on the porch, and in the wintertime, they stood inside or sat around the coal stove in the middle of the store. On this particular day, it was hot and maybe six or eight people were on the porch. As I walked up the stairs, Mr. Jackson disappeared into the store and came back with a butcher knife. It wasn't unusual to find twenty to thirty-five watermelons on the porch this time of year. And this day was no exception. He told me with a laugh to pick out a watermelon, and he would cut it. I did. He gave everybody there a slice and offered everybody who entered or left the store a slice. He said he had to be sure they were good before he sold any. Of course, everybody knew he wanted some watermelon, and being the generous person he was, he wanted to share.

Most of the people on the porch were like me. We didn't have two coins to rub together. After he served us, he went to the door and asked the two clerks to come and get a slice of melon when they had a break. Of course, everybody knew that Mr. Jackson made up boxes of food and gave them to people at Christmas and at other times when people were in need. Many people would come to the store and buy things and charge them. I often wondered if Mr. Jackson got paid for all of this.

In the wintertime, people would tell stories around the coal stove in the middle of the store. I remember Mr. Jackson telling about being in the army in World War I and going to France. He told us about his first day in the army. Just as his equipment was issued to him, someone stole it. He said he went to his sergeant and told him. Well, the sergeant looked him square in the eye and said, "Son, a good soldier never loses his equipment. Do you understand?" He laughed, "We spent a lot of time stealing each other's equipment in that war."

He also talked about the shelling and the gas and the trenches. He said three soldiers never lit cigarettes from the same match. I didn't understand that until I heard someone explaining it. They were told it gave enemy soldiers time to take aim and shoot! After that, it made sense. Mr. Jackson also talked about the mud. He said it seemed to rain every day. Then he told us how he was shot in the hip one morning when his unit had gone over the top and he was trying to help drag a wounded fellow soldier to the rear. Someone else was helping to drag him to the rear and maybe to the safety of the trenches when artillery shells went off and you could see the clouds of gas all around. He tried to put on his gas mask, but it was full of blood and mud and he didn't get it on tight enough and breathed gas into his lungs. From that day on, he could never breathe the same.

I remember the way he talked about the battlefield. No trees, no houses, nothing but mud and pools of water where the shells had fallen, there were trenches between all this. And occasionally he said you saw body parts sticking out of the mud. He said the odor was awful.

"Boys," he used to say, "there is no glory in war, only pain for those who live as well as for those who die."

One of the younger boys asked him if he ever saw any Germans. "Oh, yes, you'd see an occasional prisoner or dead Germans. They would charge our trenches and we would shoot them, or we would charge their trenches and they would shoot us." As he talked, you could tell that he had no ill feeling for the Germans. He said they didn't want to fight any more than the Americans did, and we all knew his only son was in the army in North Africa.

I hadn't wanted to fight either, and right then all I really wanted was to wiggle my toes. I thought they were moving, but I couldn't feel anything. No cold. No pain. Nothing. I wondered if I might be paralyzed. But I didn't think so. I figured I had just been in the same position too long. Even back of the crest of the hill, I could still see the light from the shells exploding in the darkness. Most of them seemed to be falling on both sides of me, not directly in front of our hill. I wondered how long it had been since I slept? I had been awake since Kelly and I talked when the shelling first started.

It was still dark, but I didn't want to let myself go and sleep. I think I was afraid I might never wake up.

Inside Mr. Jackson's store, dark-stained counters ran

down the left side of the store. On top of these were the showcases with candy. No, maybe the counters were on the right.

I was having trouble keeping anything straight, but if I tried harder, I knew I could remember. I think the soft drink cooler was on the left in front of the counter near the big front window. Behind this was sort of an office. I had been behind the counter before. There was a big black safe back there, too. Mr. Jackson used part of the counter as a desk. There was an opening in the counter between the desk area and the candy showcase, and the telephone was on the wall. This was where people who didn't have telephones made calls to relatives. They usually only did this in case of emergency. Almost no one ever called long distance or sent a telegram unless maybe someone had died. I remember hearing about the time the Japanese man came down from Washington, when a sailor from a Japanese ship had fallen overboard and drowned. The ship was carrying scrap metal from Baltimore before the war. The sailor's body was brought in by a local fishing boat and claimed by the Japanese man. He made a telephone call to Washington from Mr. Jackson's store. It was the first time any of the people hanging around the store had ever seen anyone from Japan.

Next to the candy showcase were the scales. Then came the cash register, then a tall glass jar of pickles followed by the cheese box, which contained cheese with black rind. Right there was a section of bare counter. Mr. Jackson, when he wasn't busy, liked to set a child up there and feed them this sharp delicious cheese. This was where people asked the clerks for certain items. There were shelves on the walls to the ceiling behind the counter containing almost any food item you could want—canned or dried. On the counter there was a large roll of white paper they used for wrapping packages and next to it was a large ball of string in a holder to tie them.

On the shelves behind the office area were medicines,

lamp shades, and tobacco products. I didn't know anything about the medicines, but I remembered one time my mother got a bottle of 666 and every time she took a tablespoon of the liquid she made an awful face. She told me if medicine didn't taste bad, it wouldn't do you any good. I had to remember more about the store.

The meat case was across the middle two-thirds of the back of the store. Next to it on one side were several tables with salt pork, salted hams, and shoulders. In the meat case, there was always beef. Behind it was a butcher block and a grinder for hamburger. In the wintertime, Mr. Jackson kept pans of liver pudding, scrapple, and souse cheese made from hog parts in the meat case. On top of the meat case was always a large glass jar of pickled pig's feet. On the floor in front of the meat case were wooden tubs of salted mackerel and herring and always a large tub of dried hominy.

Behind the meat case was a wall with shelves and a double door leading to an area where Mr. Jackson sold hardware—nails, hinges, some paint—and feed for chickens and hogs. Off to one side was a tank that held kerosene that people bought by the gallon and a barrel of molasses sold by the quart. In the corner was a vinegar barrel that was also sold by the quart. These large barrels had pumps, and you would turn the handles on the pumps until your container, which was brought from home, was full.

In the wintertime during hunting season, there would be rabbits hanging up. They were shipped to Baltimore six nights a week. Mr. Jackson paid twenty-five cents in cash for rabbits. You had to clean the rabbit, remove the guts, insert a stick to hold the cut sides out, and put a stick through the tendons of the hind legs to hang them up. Most kids had rabbit boxes, including myself. A rabbit box was a homemade rabbit trap. Mother and I used to catch rabbits to eat, but sometimes we sold them to Mr. Jackson. They were some kind of good, better than chicken.

Off to our right, I heard huge explosions, bigger and

louder than any of the others I had heard. Even I could tell that the shells were not coming from our rear.

Kelly crawled up behind me and said, "Those loud explosions are from our naval guns. There must be something big going on. It's time for me to check with the lieutenant. Four eyes might be better than two. Just hold on, kid. Maybe we can get you out of here today."

I didn't know whether Kelly thought I was about to bleed to death or what. It scared me that he had said, "Hold on." I knew I was getting weak, but I was, for sure, going to hold on. I knew I had to stay awake. I couldn't have slept with all that noise anyway.

Okay, what did the rest of the store look like? All down the right side were showcases of perfume, and powder and clothes for men and women and boxes of shoes and boots. I could just see Pamela Hill behind the counter.

I thought about the time I was to meet her at the PX and go to a movie. As I entered the PX, she came toward me and said she wouldn't be able to go out with me. She had to finish taking inventory.

"How about tomorrow night?" I said.

Her face turned a little red as she said, "I have dates the next two nights, and then I go back to school."

I'm afraid she really didn't want to go out with me. But, boy, I wish she had! I never saw her again. . .

In the front of the store, was a large produce case just as big as the meat case with all kinds of fruits and vegetables. I remember selling wild blackberries to Mr. Jackson and getting ten cents a quart for them.

The coal stove was in the center of the store, near a rack with boxes of cookies and racks containing bakery bread, all sliced. Sitting in that foxhole I would have given almost anything to have just one of those cookies. I had to stay awake. If I had a cookie, it would help, although I couldn't sleep, the shelling was so loud, except after a while, I didn't seem to hear anything.

Kelly crawled to the edge of the foxhole and asked how I was. I told him I was doing okay. He was pretty excited. He had talked to the lieutenant and they thought we would be relieved shortly, then they could get me to medical care. The lieutenant thought something was happening. There was no sign of enemy forces advancing toward us, but he expected to see them anytime now. Kelly suggested I try to get some sleep. He said it would be daylight soon. I asked Kelly how could the lieutenant see the enemy coming if it was dark. He said with all the shells exploding, it was just like daylight.

As I shut my eyes, and if I thought real hard I could picture some of the people who hung around the store. They were real characters.

Commodore Keeve was a middle-aged black man who called himself a tree surgeon. He made a living topping trees, cutting up wood for people, white-washing fences, and selling beauty products. What a combination! He also was a scholar of the Bible, and they said he could preach a wonderful sermon. I think his name was Job, but everybody called him Commodore. People talked in low tones and said he had been in a mental institution, but who knew if this was true? Around the stove in the store at night, Mr. Jackson and others would ask him questions about the Bible, and Commodore Keeve would give explanations that sounded good.

Another frequent visitor to the store was Airplane Payne. This young black man loved to fly. The only time he had ever been up in an airplane was after World War I. Someone came to Truitt's farm and carried passengers for five dollars. Payne spent all his money on plane rides. After that experience, he cut all the airplane pictures he could find from newspapers and magazines, and he built his own plane. It was said that he tied the plane up a tree, started the motor, and cut the rope holding the plane. Of course he crashed, but he didn't get hurt. Later, he got the plane operating so that he could drive it around a field. I don't think he ever did get it to fly. All the people at the store used to tease him about flying, but he enjoyed the attention, and the truth was everyone thought he was amazing to build a plane out of scrap material.

He also loved to carve figures of people and places he had seen. He built beautiful models of boats he had worked on. He built everything from scraps. I heard him say one time that he had only been as far as second grade, that he couldn't learn. He said the teachers just had to knock it into his head.

I always thought he had learned a whole lot.

Chapter Eighteen

I must have fallen asleep because when I opened my eyes, there was light, but no sun. The sound of the shells exploding was still almost constant. At first I was afraid because I didn't know what was happening. Where were Kelly and the lieutenant? Had they left me? I didn't believe they had—I knew they were busy at the observation post—but I was alone and helpless.

Again, I tried to think of home; I had some good friends like Captain Ed. In my hometown, across the intersection from the store was Captain Ed's service station. The post office was in one end of the building with a separate entrance. Listening to some of the boys in the barracks talk, I knew it was not a "service" station exactly. Most people put in their own gas. Of course, sometimes Captain Ed, the proprietor, would help them, but he was usually busy waiting on people. The station sold groceries, candy, and ice cream. There was a room on the right with clothes for sale. This was Captain Ed's wife's project. One of her earlier projects had been a lunch room in a room to the left. Captain Ed and his wife lived in the back of the station.

There was a group of people who used to hang around the station and talk about the course of the war, fishing prospects and the local economy. They drank pop and ate peanuts and threw the hulls on the floor. Captain Ed fussed all the time about having to sweep up, but he never told anyone not to throw the hulls on the floor. Captain Ed was well versed in many subjects and never at a loss for words. In the evening after the news broadcasts were over someone would always talk him into playing his violin. He could do country fiddling or he could play the fancy pieces he had learned as a student.

One evening after he played "Turkey in the Straw," he told us about the salesman who sold his father an interest in some oil wells in Oklahoma. They never produced any oil, and in the end his father lost his entire investment which was his life savings. He talked about the loss quite a bit. He must have had a hard time growing up, since his family ended up very poor.

A frequent customer at Captain Ed's was a black man named Penrod. Penrod couldn't count too well and often bought ingredients for tomato wine, a homemade brew. He needed five pounds of sugar, six cans of tomatoes, and two yeast cakes. I never saw anybody make it, but from all reports, it was good. Anyway Penrod would ask Captain Ed for one ingredient and pay for it. Then he would look at his money and ask for the next ingredient. After Captain Ed had gotten an item and Penrod had paid, Captain Ed put it in a bag. As soon as Captain Ed would sit down on a bench and join in the conversation, Penrod would ask for another ingredient. After several purchases, when Penrod asked for something else, Captain Ed would tell him, "Not another damn thing, Penrod!" Penrod would leave in a huff, but he was satisfied with his purchases, and he always returned. In fact, Penrod was one of Captain Ed's most regular customers.

Another funny thing about Penrod was the way he would go to the post office and ask Jay's mother, Mrs. Hopkins, to tell him how old he was. This seems funny, but Penrod couldn't remember too well. Penrod had been born in a tenant house on a farm owned by Mrs. Hopkins' parents. This made her his authority. Time and again, she would tell him the month, day, and year of his birth.

As he left, he always said, "Thanks, I'll remember it this time."

When the lunch room was open, it had a jukebox. On Friday nights, high school kids use to come there and dance. Captain Ed would open the jukebox and give them the nickels that were already in the box so they could play more records. He wasn't as interested in making money as he was in entertaining the kids. Of course, the kids bought ice cream, pop, and candy while they were there, and most of the parents of the kids were Captain Ed's friends and customers.

I was a little young for this dancing, but I liked to watch. One time, one of the boys had driven his father's car there and offered to take me home. Mother and I were living in an old house off a dirt road about a mile away. I didn't get a chance to ride in a car very often, so I accepted the ride.

A couple of other boys got in the car to ride along. Billy, the driver, decided to take the long way, which was a little farther, but the curved, unpaved road was very sandy. As we came around the first turn, the car got away from Billy and turned over on its side. Luckily, no one was hurt, but we had a little trouble opening the door. With the car on its side, the door had to be opened upward.

It took a lot of pushing but we soon got out. There wasn't even any broken glass. Billy and his pals decided to walk back to Captain Ed's and get help, but I decided I'd better get on home. I sure didn't want to hang around and hear what Billy's father would say to him.

The lieutenant stuck his head over my foxhole and peered down. "How are you doing?"

"Okay, I guess," I said.

Then he asked me if I was cold and reminded me that I was not supposed to eat or drink.

I told him I wasn't too cold and I wouldn't eat.

He cautioned me to stay under cover and keep warm. "We can't have you going into shock, you know." Shells exploded on both sides of us. "I think we're going to get out of here today," he added. We haven't had any word yet, nor have we seen any sign of an attack, but I believe something big is going on. Either our forces will advance or the enemy will attack." Then he said, "Don't worry. Sergeant Kelly and I will carry you back to our lines if necessary." He patted my shoulder and told me to hang in there. He said they would get me back to our lines where I would get medical treatment—if our forces didn't advance. He also told me that he was going back to help Sergeant Kelly and one of them would keep checking on me. If any word came, he said, they would let me know. "Stay down in that foxhole, private. You never know about a stray artillery shell."

I tried to smile at him as he slipped away. I knew better than he about those stray artillery shells.

Chapter Nineteen

The next thing I remembered Kelly was tugging at my shoulder. At first I didn't understand what he was saying, but then everything came back to me. He just wanted to know if I was all right.

It took me a while, but I told him I thought so. He said he had had a hard time waking me up, and I asked him why he wanted to. He was the one who had told me to get some rest.

"Well, you can't sleep all day," he said.

He also told me no word had come for us to leave the post. I looked up at the sky. The sun was shining, but it seemed even colder than before. I asked Kelly if he and the lieutenant had seen anything.

"Nothing but exploding shells. The shelling is intense and seems to come from both sides. Then it stops for a few minutes."

This must have been one of the quiet times because I didn't hear any shells exploding. Kelly said the lieutenant had sent him back to check on me and now he had to go back to the observation post.

I knew I was weaker, but how could I help it? I hadn't had any food and only a little water to wet my lips. I tried to

123

move the hand that was on the compress, but I couldn't. It was numb, so I gave up. Maybe the bleeding had stopped. I sure didn't want it to start again.

Right then the shells began exploding to our far right. They were the big ones, the kind Kelly thought were from our navy ships. There wasn't anything I could do anyway. I couldn't move or anything, so I tried not to think about it.

Kelly had probably thought I was dead or unconscious, but I was still holding on. I could take it. They would get me back, and I would make it.

The sun was milk-white like chalk dust covered it or something. It had been like that the last time I saw Uncle Henderson Locust. Jay and I went to visit him. He wasn't my real uncle, but a real old black man who lived near us. As children we were taught to call older black people "aunt" and "uncle." Mother said it showed respect.

This man was tall, with a big frame, but he had no fat on him. In his younger days he must have been a giant. Sometimes, in the summertime, he sat under a huge red oak tree in his yard during the heat of the day. He told us that tree had been almost as large when he was a slave as it was when he sat there telling tales. He said he and his family had been owned by people on a nearby farm. After the war, when they were freed, they had moved near by. He told us how he used to sit under this tree and watched sheep graze when he was a slave boy. He told us how he had said, "One day I would like to live near this tree." He smiled and said, "and I got to live here."

He told us he couldn't do much work anymore, just grow a few 'taters and some tobacco for chewing.

We asked him if he ever had a wife.

"Yes, but she is gone to heaven now, and most of my children, too. The last time I heard, I still had two girls living in Baltimore, but you know I can't write much. And I can't read." He frowned. "You boys best get all the education you can."

124

"You know," he said as he turned to Jay, "your mama reads my letters to me and she writes what I tell her to say, too. She is a nice lady. After she reads me my letters, I take them home and put them with my Bible and the picture of my wife. I keep both them near my bed." He raised his arm stiffly and pointed toward the house.

Jay asked, "How many children did you have?"

Tilting his head back and closing his eyes, he said, "I had six boys and six girls. Four died before they got grown.

"You know, these old eyes don't see so good anymore, but I like to talk anyway. I don't know much about what's going on now, but I know about the past. Now, all they talk about is war. They had a war a few years ago, you know, and they said it was a war to end all wars. But they was wrong, Now they is fighting again. I hate to see all these young boys go in the army. Some of them ain't coming home no more either."

He frowned and looked down at the ground, "Two of my older brothers ran away to the North. They said they was going to join the Union Army, but we never heard from then again. Maybe they did. And maybe got killed, too."

I asked, "How old are you, Uncle Henderson?"

With a big smile, he said, "I don't rightly know, but I was about your size when the war started."

When Jay asked him what he had done for a living, he said he took down trees and grubbed up the stumps to make more farmland.

"You know, people used to cut down trees, and I would grub up the stumps by hand. All I ever used was a ax and a hoe. Can't do much of that anymore. My knees don't move none. But I still work my 'taters and tobacco if I do it early morning. Sometimes I'm asleep before it's dark in the summertime, but at the first light, I'm awake and ready for breakfast. I can cook a little, and nothing tastes better than my fried fat back and hotcakes. Sometimes I fry an egg in the grease, and I like to put the grease drippings on my hotcakes. It sure tastes good."

Before we left, we asked him if there was anything we could do for him.

"No, I don't guess so. I am still able to cut my own wood, and I get to the store and the post office every now and then. Mr. Jackson usually brings me home or finds me a ride. He is such a nice man."

Then he looked at us with a smile and said, "Have you boys ever walked to the cemetery?"

"No," I answered. We knew he meant the black cemetery.

"Well," he said, "sometime when you want to take a walk, you go see about my family's graves. I want to know what shape my wife's stone is in."

We asked him where his lot was.

He smiled real big and said proudly, "My lot's on the point at the top of the hill, and you see the water from there. Just follow the road to the end and you can't miss it."

We assured him we would check his lot for him and let him know if everything was all right, then we told him good-bye and started toward my house.

As we walked up the dirt road in silence, Jay suggested we go to the cemetery right then. He said he had been there with his father to funerals and that it was a beautiful place.

Jay didn't have to be home until 1:00 P.M. because his mother worked and lunch wouldn't be until she got home. Since it was not far from where I lived, we started off. It was a beautiful sunny day. Kind of on the warm side, but not too bad for August. We were walking along the dirt road talking about not much of anything, when we noticed a man approaching.

Before long, we could see it was Mr. Jasper. He was a regular around the stove at Mr. Jackson's store in the wintertime. But during the summer, he farmed and worked on the water. He was a good story teller, but the story we always liked best was the tale he told about going to court.

Mr. Jasper was a tenant farmer. He didn't own the land he worked or the house he lived in. We didn't know what rent he paid or what share of his crop he gave the landowner, but times were hard for everyone, and a lot of farmers had lost their land and homes.

Well, for some reason, Mr. Jasper had to move to another farm. Anyway, he wanted to take his manure to his new place. Tenant farmers couldn't afford to buy commercial fertilizer, so they used natural fertilizer on their crops and manure was a real asset. The landowner told him that he couldn't move it because it was real estate, but Mr. Jasper said he didn't see why he couldn't move his manure.

Eventually, the issue went to county court with Mr. Jasper acting as his own lawyer. The landowner said he could move his cows, horses, hens, hay, and feed, but not the manure. So Mr. Jasper said he wanted to ask the judge a couple of questions. He said he didn't have much education, but asked the judge if his livestock was his personal property.

The judge said, "Yes, that's correct."

Then Mr. Jasper said, "My hay and feed are personal property, aren't they, Judge?"

The judge answered, "Yes, they are personal property."

"Well, Judge, I don't understand how personal property can eat personal property but what comes out is real estate."

The judge looked surprised, but he ruled that Mr. Jasper could remove his manure.

As we walked on down the dusty road, the breeze picked up. It made an occasional dust devil. The wind picked up the dust and blew it around in a circle like a tiny tornado. It would have been hot if the wind hadn't been blowing.

We turned off on an old lane, full of weeds, with deep holes, and ruts. As dry as it was, green water was still standing in the deeper holes. We walked passed several houses down that lane. Commodore Keeve lived in one of them. On the right, there was a road that went to a landing where several people kept their work boats.

Jay knew the cemetery would be straight ahead, and as we entered an area of large oak and pine trees, we could see the tombstones. On some graves, there were hand-carved wooden markers. It felt funny to walk on this shady road, like I was in the presence of all these dead people. But still, it was a beautiful place.

We remembered that Uncle Henderson Locust had told us his lot was at the end of the road, so we kept walking. Along the way we saw an interesting grave stone. When we looked at the dates, we couldn't believe it. The person was born in 1817 and she died in 1933. Can you believe it? One hundred and sixteen years old. Maybe someone had made a mistake. Jay said he had heard Commodore Keeve say something about this lady one time. Supposedly, she had five husbands and about twenty children. By the time she died, all her husbands and children were dead, but she had grandchildren, great grandchildren, and even some great-great greats.

Along the narrow road, were stones and carved markers. The road turned slowly and went back to meet the road coming in, like a circle. This was how the hearses and cars turned around. Down there, at the end was the most beautiful part. Every way we turned, we could see water. It was so beautiful up there on that hilltop. Below us, the land sloped gently to the water. No wonder Uncle Henderson had smiled as he talked about the cemetery. I remember we poked at each other and said maybe when we died they would bury us here.

After being struck with the beauty of the hill, we hurried to find Uncle Henderson's lot. There it was, straight ahead, just as he had told us. There was a stone marking his wife's grave. We figured it out. She had been dead nearly forty years. There were also markers of three of his children.

Kelly crawled back up to my foxhole. There was a big smile on his face. He said, "The lieutenant just got orders to move back through the unit we passed on our approach to hill 4413."

I wanted to smile, but I couldn't. I felt so weak.

Kelly said, "Don't worry, kid. You don't even have to walk. We'll carry you."

Chapter Twenty

When the lieutenant got up to my foxhole, he said, "How are you doing, kid," and he smiled. Then he said, "Kelly and I are going to carry you back. Just hold on."

He told Kelly the plan, "We'll make a stretcher using two poles from something. We can carry our guns and whatever equipment we can. Take a rock and bash the radio and the BC scope. Maybe we can use the legs from the BC scope for the stretcher poles."

Kelly protested a little. "How are we going to account for this stuff?" he asked "I'm signed out for these things."

"Don't you know? A rock hit that radio and wrecked it? The boulder got the BC scope, too. The important thing is we don't want the enemy to capture these things. What's most important—this boy's life or a few pieces of equipment? Go on. Use the legs off the scope for a stretcher. I'll take care of it with the supply officer." he looked at his watch, "We want to get back before dark. I don't look forward to going through our lines in the dark. One of us has already been hit by friendly fire. We don't want to make it three of us.

"Remember, Kelly, most of our walking is going to be downhill. You're the tallest, so lead the way. After we get to level ground, I'll get in front. We must not shake this boy any more than we have to."

The lieutenant looked at me, and said, "He's weak, but he's going to make it."

I thought, what nice people the lieutenant and Kelly were. Maybe I would make it. They were sure trying to help me.

I knew this would be the end of the war for me. I had heard other soldiers talk about being wounded and going to a hospital in Japan, but this was just talk. I don't think any of them had really been wounded.

I was so weak, my legs were numb—also my hand. I wondered if I would I start bleeding again. But actually I wasn't sure I had even stopped bleeding. I knew lying on the stretcher as we went down the rocky hill wouldn't be easy, even if the lieutenant and Kelly were careful and didn't fall. There wasn't anything I could do but try not to roll off the stretcher.

I was thinking it might be easier if I passed out, when I heard a sudden crash. Apparently Kelly had brought the radio and the BC scope from the foxholes on the far side of the hill to the rear, and he was wrecking them. I heard the lieutenant tell Kelly to be sure all the tubes in the radio were broken and to smash all the other parts so they wouldn't be of use to the enemy.

Kelly said he was going to take the legs off of the scope before he broke the lens and other parts. The lieutenant said, "Don't be easy on it. Just do it. We've got no time to waste."

Kelly asked the lieutenant what to do with the food we had left.

"Just put it in a foxhole and throw rocks on it. Let's move out. We'll use the blankets and ponchos to make the stretcher. I think the kid will rest better if he isn't concerned about falling off."

Kelly said, "The walk down this hill won't be easy, but it will be better than when we came up it in the dark."

In a few minutes, everything was ready. I saw Kelly hit

the head of the scope against a large sharp boulder, and I saw pieces fly in all directions. Together they fastened blankets and ponchos on the legs of the BC scope. The lieutenant bent over me and said, "I think we're ready."

He and Kelly slung their weapons over one shoulder. Kelly asked if their safeties should be on.

The lieutenant said, "Yes. There is a round in the chamber and a full clip, but with both hands on the stretcher, we won't have time to shoot if we meet an enemy patrol. They might take us prisoner or shoot us. I don't know. We just have to take that chance. If one of us falls down, the other may also. That could cause our weapons to discharge and would alert any enemy patrol in the area. And we might shoot ourselves or each other."

Kelly said, "I'll get his feet." The lieutenant put his hands under my arms and they slowly lifted me. The pain was awful. I must have passed out. The next thing I remember I was flat on the stretcher with blankets over me. I could hear the lieutenant call me, but he seemed far away. I could have been dreaming, I guess. Finally, I must have said something because Kelly told me I was going to be okay. I felt better, I thought, but the earth below was spinning and I felt like I was falling.

As I turned my head, I caught the lieutenant's eye. I said, "Lieutenant Brown . . . promise me if I don't make it and you do, that you will see my mother in North Carolina when you get home to the states. That's where she lives now. You can get my records. Just tell her I tried to do what I was told. Tell her I love her."

Lieutenant Brown looked down at me with a serious expression on his face and said, "I'll do what you ask, but you are going to be home before I am. Now, just think of something pleasant."

"Think about Virginia," Kelly added. "We will have you back in your old state in no time."

I heard the lieutenant ask Kelly if he was ready.

Kelly said, "Yes."

"Okay, pick up on the count of three." And I was off. I tried to think of pretty, sunny days in Virginia, but what I remembered was the day my dog, Lollipop, died. I was sixteen. She was old—about eight, I guess. We never had any good food for her, but I used to share mine with her. She hadn't eaten for several days near the end, and we didn't have money to take her to a veterinarian, so all I could do was hold her in my lap and pet her head. She just seemed to go to sleep.

I wondered if death would be like that for me. I knew the lieutenant and Kelly would be as easy as they could, but every step was agonizing pain, and there was blood on my hand. It felt warm, but what could I do?

I kept passing out for a while, then regaining consciousness, but the pain. . . I didn't hear the lieutenant and Kelly say anything, but I could tell they were walking. I could hear their shoes hit the rocks. Then I heard the lieutenant say that the ground was level and he would get in front.

After a time, they were talking to someone. I guess our front lines had been told to expect us to be coming through. Two people replaced the lieutenant and Kelly, and I could hear them talking about the aid station. I looked around, and saw the sun setting behind the hills.

Then we entered a tent. It must have been the aid station. I could hear the lieutenant and Kelly talking to a doctor. They were trying to tell him where I was hit. I felt the blanket and poncho being pulled off me. I also felt someone reach for my dog tag and yell out my blood type. I felt a prick in my arm after someone was told to cut my jacket. I was so sleepy. I could hear someone tell Lieutenant Brown and Kelly that I had lost too much blood, that I wouldn't make it. I thought maybe I would go to sleep like my dog, Lollipop.

The lieutenant was whispering, but I could hear him say, "Here's this kid, been in the army five months. Been in